DOVER ☆ CHILDREN'S THRIFT CLASSICS

Mowgli Stories from "The Jungle Book"

RUDYARD KIPLING

Illustrated by Thea Kliros

D1004745

DOVER PUBLICATIONS, INC.
New York

DOVER CHILDREN'S THRIFT CLASSICS

EDITOR OF THIS VOLUME: THOMAS CROFTS

Copyright

Published in Canada by General Publishing Company, Ltd., 30 Lesmill Road, Don Mills, Toronto, Ontario.

Published in the United Kingdom by Constable and Company, Ltd., 3 The Lanchesters, 162–164 Fulham Palace Road, London W6 9ER.

Bibliographical Note

Mowgli Stories from "The Jungle Book" is a new selection of three stories from *The Jungle Book*, first published by The Century Co., New York, 1894. The stories are printed here unabridged. A new introductory Note, as well as new illustrations by Thea Kliros, have been specially prepared for this edition.

Library of Congress Cataloging-in-Publication Data

Kipling, Rudyard, 1865–1936.
    Mowgli stories from "The jungle book" / Rudyard Kipling.
       p.   cm. — (Dover children's thrift classics)
    "A new selection . . . from The jungle book, first published by the Century Co., New York, 1894. The stories are printed here unabridged. A new introductory note, as well as new illustrations by Thea Kliros, have been specially prepared for this edition"—T.p. verso.
    Contents: Mowgli's brothers—Kaa's hunting—Tiger! Tiger!
    Summary: Includes several adventures of Mowgli, the boy reared by a pack of wolves in an Indian jungle.
    ISBN 0-486-28030-6 (pbk.)
    1. Mowgli (Fictitious character)—Juvenile fiction. [1. Jungles—Fiction.   2. Animals—Fiction.   3. India—Fiction.] I. Kliros, Thea, ill.   II. Kipling, Rudyard, 1865–1936. Jungle book. Selections. 1994.   III. Title.   IV. Series.
[Fic]—dc20
                                         94–467
                                          CIP
                                          AC

Manufactured in the United States of America
Dover Publications, Inc., 31 East 2nd Street, Mineola, N.Y. 11501

Note

RUDYARD KIPLING, who lived from 1865 to 1936, wrote novels, short stories, poetry and children's tales. His folkish yarns about India (where the author was born) are among his most famous and widely read writings for children, holding at the same time an undeniable fascination for adults. Kipling, a great traveler and staunch advocate of British imperialism, reposed and wrote in British-ruled India and South Africa, among other places. His tales both affirmed his nationalistic convictions and cultivated in his readers an appreciation of the exotic, the strange and even the savage, the children's stories not excepted.

The tales in this volume comprise all three Mowgli stories from Kipling's *The Jungle Book*, a collection of tales set in India which appeared in 1894. (*The Second Jungle Book*, which has more Mowgli stories, was published in 1895.) Mowgli, the boy raised by wolves, is the most famous of the many *Jungle Book* characters. In these three episodes we glimpse Mowgli's infancy ("Mowgli's Brothers"), his boyhood and education in the Jungle ("Kaa's Hunting") and the beginning of his manhood (" 'Tiger! Tiger!' ")

Those who are familiar with Rudyard Kipling's masterful story-telling will be eager to peruse these tales again; those who are not are in for a treat.

Contents

List of Illustrations

Mowgli's Brothers

Now Rann, the Kite, brings home the night
    That Mang, the Bat, sets free—
The herds are shut in byre and hut,
    For loosed till dawn are we.
This is the hour of pride and power,
    Talon and tush and claw.
Oh, hear the call!—Good hunting all
    That keep the Jungle Law!

Night-Song in the Jungle.

Mowgli's Brothers

IT WAS SEVEN O'CLOCK of a very warm evening in the Seeonee hills when Father Wolf woke up from his day's rest, scratched himself, yawned, and spread out his paws one after the other to get rid of the sleepy feeling in the tips. Mother Wolf lay with her big gray nose dropped across her four tumbling, squealing cubs, and the moon shone into the mouth of the cave where they all lived. "Augrh!" said Father Wolf, "it is time to hunt again"; and he was going to spring downhill when a little shadow with a bushy tail crossed the threshold and whined: "Good luck go with you, O Chief of the Wolves; and good luck and strong white teeth go with the noble children, that they may never forget the hungry in this world."

It was the jackal—Tabaqui, the Dish-licker—and the wolves of India despise Tabaqui because he runs about making mischief, and telling tales, and eating rags and

pieces of leather from the village rubbish-
heaps. They are afraid of him too, because
Tabaqui, more than any one else in the jungle,
is apt to go mad, and then he forgets that he
was ever afraid of any one, and runs through
the forest biting everything in his way. Even
the tiger hides when little Tabaqui goes mad,
for madness is the most disgraceful thing
that can overtake a wild creature. We call it
hydrophobia, but they call it *dewanee*—the
madness—and run.

"Enter, then, and look," said Father Wolf,
stiffly; "but there is no food here."

"For a wolf, no," said Tabaqui; "but for so
mean a person as myself a dry bone is a good
feast. Who are we, the Gidur-log [the Jackal
People], to pick and choose?" He scuttled to
the back of the cave, where he found the bone
of a buck with some meat on it, and sat crack-
ing the end merrily.

"All thanks for this good meal," he said,
licking his lips. "How beautiful are the noble
children! How large are their eyes! And so
young too! Indeed, indeed, I might have
remembered that the children of kings are
men from the beginning."

Now, Tabaqui knew as well as any one else
that there is nothing so unlucky as to compliment children to their faces; and it pleased

him to see Mother and Father Wolf look uncomfortable.

Tabaqui sat still, rejoicing in the mischief that he had made, and then he said spitefully:

"Shere Khan, the Big One, has shifted his hunting-grounds. He will hunt among these hills during the next moon, so he has told me."

Shere Khan was the tiger who lived near the Waingunga River, twenty miles away.

"He has no right!" Father Wolf began angrily. "By the Law of the Jungle he has no right to change his quarters without fair warning. He will frighten every head of game within ten miles; and I—I have to kill for two, these days."

"His mother did not call him Lungri [the Lame One] for nothing," said Mother Wolf, quietly. "He has been lame in one foot from his birth. That is why he has only killed cattle. Now the villagers of the Waingunga are angry with him, and he has come here to make *our* villagers angry. They will scour the jungle for him when he is far away, and we and our children must run when the grass is set alight. Indeed, we are very grateful to Shere Khan!"

"Shall I tell him of your gratitude?" said Tabaqui.

"Out!" snapped Father Wolf. "Out, and hunt

with thy master. Thou hast done harm enough for one night."

"I go," said Tabaqui, quietly. "Ye can hear Shere Khan below in the thickets. I might have saved myself the message."

Father Wolf listened, and in the dark valley that ran down to a little river, he heard the dry, angry, snarly, singsong whine of a tiger who has caught nothing and does not care if all the jungle knows it.

"The fool!" said Father Wolf. "To begin a night's work with that noise! Does he think that our buck are like his fat Waingunga bullocks?"

"H'sh! It is neither bullock nor buck that he hunts to-night," said Mother Wolf; "it is Man." The whine had changed to a sort of humming purr that seemed to roll from every quarter of the compass. It was the noise that bewilders wood-cutters, and gipsies sleeping in the open, and makes them run sometimes into the very mouth of the tiger.

"Man!" said Father Wolf, showing all his white teeth. "Faugh! Are there not enough beetles and frogs in the tanks that he must eat Man—and on our ground too!"

The Law of the Jungle, which never orders anything without a reason, forbids every beast to eat Man except when he is killing to show his children how to kill, and then he must hunt outside the hunting-grounds of his pack or tribe. The real reason for this is that man-killing means, sooner or later, the arrival of white men on elephants, with guns, and hundreds of brown men with gongs and rockets and torches. Then everybody in the jungle suffers. The reason the beasts give among themselves is that Man is the weakest and most defenseless of all living things, and it is unsportsmanlike to touch him. They say too—and it is true—that man-eaters become mangy, and lose their teeth.

The purr grew louder, and ended in the full-throated "Aaarh!" of the tiger's charge.

Then there was a howl—an untigerish howl—from Shere Khan. "He has missed," said Mother Wolf. "What is it?"

Father Wolf ran out a few paces and heard Shere Khan muttering and mumbling savagely, as he tumbled about in the scrub.

"The fool has had no more sense than to jump at a wood-cutters' camp-fire, so he has burned his feet," said Father Wolf, with a grunt. "Tabaqui is with him."

"Something is coming uphill," said Mother Wolf, twitching one ear. "Get ready."

The bushes rustled a little in the thicket, and Father Wolf dropped with his haunches under him, ready for his leap. Then, if you had been watching, you would have seen the most wonderful thing in the world—the wolf checked in mid-spring. He made his bound before he saw what it was he was jumping at, and then he tried to stop himself. The result was that he shot up straight into the air for four or five feet, landing almost where he left ground.

"Man!" he snapped. "A man's cub. Look!"

Directly in front of him, holding on by a low branch, stood a naked brown baby who could just walk—as soft and as dimpled a little thing as ever came to a wolf's cave at night. He looked up into Father Wolf's face and laughed.

"Is that a man's cub?" said Mother Wolf. "I have never seen one. Bring it here."

A wolf accustomed to moving his own cubs can, if necessary, mouth an egg without breaking it, and though Father Wolf's jaws closed right on the child's back not a tooth even scratched the skin, as he laid it down among the cubs.

"How little! How naked, and—how bold!" said Mother Wolf, softly. The baby was pushing his way between the cubs to get close to the warm hide. "Ahai! He is taking his meal with the others. And so this is a man's cub.

Now, was there ever a wolf that could boast
of a man's cub among her children?"

"I have heard now and again of such a
thing, but never in our pack or in my time,"
said Father Wolf. "He is altogether without
hair, and I could kill him with a touch of my
foot. But see, he looks up and is not afraid."

The moonlight was blocked out of the
mouth of the cave, for Shere Khan's great
square head and shoulders were thrust into
the entrance. Tabaqui, behind him, was
squeaking: "My Lord, my Lord, it went in
here!"

"Shere Khan does us great honor," said
Father Wolf, but his eyes were very angry.
"What does Shere Khan need?"

"My quarry. A man's cub went this way,"
said Shere Khan. "Its parents have run off.
Give it to me."

Shere Khan had jumped at a wood-cutter's
camp-fire, as Father Wolf had said, and was
furious from the pain of his burned feet. But
Father Wolf knew that the mouth of the cave
was too narrow for a tiger to come in by. Even
where he was, Shere Khan's shoulders and
fore paws were cramped for want of room,
as a man's would be if he tried to fight in a
barrel.

"The Wolves are a free people," said Father

Wolf. "They take orders from the Head of the Pack, and not from any striped cattle-killer. The man's cub is ours—to kill if we choose."

"Ye choose and ye do not choose! What talk is this of choosing? By the Bull that I killed, am I to stand nosing into your dog's den for my fair dues? It is I, Shere Khan, who speak!"

The tiger's roar filled the cave with thunder. Mother Wolf shook herself clear of the cubs and sprang forward, her eyes, like two green moons in the darkness, facing the blazing eyes of Shere Khan.

"And it is I, Raksha [the Demon], who answer. The man's cub is mine, Lungri—mine to me! He shall not be killed. He shall live to run with the Pack and to hunt with the Pack; and in the end, look you, hunter of little naked cubs—frog-eater—fish-killer, he shall hunt *thee!* Now get hence, or by the Sambhur that I killed (*I* eat no starved cattle), back thou goest to thy mother, burned beast of the jungle, lamer than ever thou camest into the world! Go!"

Father Wolf looked on amazed. He had almost forgotten the days when he won Mother Wolf in fair fight from five other wolves, when she ran in the Pack and was not called the Demon for compliment's sake. Shere Khan might have faced Father Wolf, but he could not stand up against Mother Wolf, for he knew that where he was she had all the advantage of the ground, and would fight to the death. So he backed out of the cave-mouth growling, and when he was clear he shouted:

"Each dog barks in his own yard! We will see what the Pack will say to this fostering of man-cubs. The cub is mine, and to my teeth he will come in the end, O bush-tailed thieves!"

Mother Wolf threw herself down panting among the cubs, and Father Wolf said to her gravely:

"Shere Khan speaks this much truth. The cub must be shown to the Pack. Wilt thou still keep him, Mother?"

"Keep him!" she gasped. "He came naked, by night, alone and very hungry; yet he was not afraid! Look, he has pushed one of my babes to one side already. And that lame butcher would have killed him, and would have run off to the Waingunga while the villagers here hunted through all our lairs in revenge! Keep him? Assuredly I will keep him. Lie still, little frog. O thou Mowgli—for Mowgli, the Frog, I will call thee,—the time will come when thou wilt hunt Shere Khan as he has hunted thee!"

"But what will our Pack say?" said Father Wolf.

The Law of the Jungle lays down very

clearly that any wolf may, when he marries, withdraw from the Pack he belongs to; but as soon as his cubs are old enough to stand on their feet he must bring them to the Pack Council, which is generally held once a month at full moon, in order that the other wolves may identify them. After that inspection the cubs are free to run where they please, and until they have killed their first buck no excuse is accepted if a grown wolf of the Pack kills one of them. The punishment is death where the murderer can be found; and if you think for a minute you will see that this must be so.

Father Wolf waited till his cubs could run a little, and then on the night of the Pack Meeting took them and Mowgli and Mother Wolf to the Council Rock—a hilltop covered with stones and boulders where a hundred wolves could hide. Akela, the great gray Lone Wolf, who led all the Pack by strength and cunning, lay out at full length on his rock, and below him sat forty or more wolves of every size and color, from badger-colored veterans who could handle a buck alone, to young black three-year-olds who thought they could. The Lone Wolf had led them for a year now. He had fallen twice into a wolf-trap in his youth, and once he had been beaten and left for

Council Rock—a hilltop covered with stones and
boulders where a hundred wolves could hide.

dead; so he knew the manners and customs of men.

There was very little talking at the Rock. The cubs tumbled over one another in the center of the circle where their mothers and fathers sat, and now and again a senior wolf would go quietly up to a cub, look at him carefully, and return to his place on noiseless feet. Sometimes a mother would push her cub far out into the moonlight, to be sure that he had not been overlooked. Akela from his rock would cry: "Ye know the Law—ye know the Law! Look well, O Wolves!" And the anxious mothers would take up the call: "Look—look well, O Wolves!"

At last—and Mother Wolf's neck-bristles lifted as the time came—Father Wolf pushed "Mowgli, the Frog," as they called him, into the center, where he sat laughing and playing with some pebbles that glistened in the moonlight.

Akela never raised his head from his paws, but went on with the monotonous cry, "Look well!" A muffled roar came up from behind the rocks—the voice of Shere Khan crying, "The cub is mine; give him to me. What have the Free People to do with a man's cub?"

Akela never even twitched his ears. All he said was, "Look well, O Wolves! What have the Free People to do with the orders of any save the Free People? Look well!"

There was a chorus of deep growls, and a young wolf in his fourth year flung back Shere Khan's question to Akela: "What have the Free People to do with a man's cub?"

Now the Law of the Jungle lays down that if there is any dispute as to the right of a cub to be accepted by the Pack, he must be spoken for by at least two members of the Pack who are not his father and mother.

"Who speaks for this cub?" said Akela. "Among the Free People, who speaks?" There was no answer, and Mother Wolf got ready for what she knew would be her last fight, if things came to fighting.

Then the only other creature who is allowed at the Pack Council—Baloo, the sleepy brown bear who teaches the wolf cubs the Law of the Jungle; old Baloo—who can come and go where he pleases because he eats only nuts and roots and honey—rose up on his hind quarters and grunted.

"The man's cub—the man's cub?" he said. "*I* speak for the man's cub. There is no harm in a man's cub. I have no gift of words, but I speak the truth. Let him run with the Pack, and be entered with the others. I myself will teach him."

"We need yet another," said Akela. "Baloo has spoken, and he is our teacher for the young cubs. Who speaks besides Baloo?"

A black shadow dropped down into the circle. It was Bagheera, the Black Panther, inky black all over, but with the panther markings showing up in certain lights like the pattern of watered silk. Everybody knew Bagheera, and nobody cared to cross his path; for he was as cunning as Tabaqui, as bold as the wild buffalo, and as reckless as the wounded elephant. But he had a voice as soft as wild honey dripping from a tree, and a skin softer than down.

"O Akela, and ye, the Free People," he purred, "I have no right in your assembly; but the Law of the Jungle says that if there is a doubt which is not a killing matter in regard to a new cub, the life of that cub may be bought at a price. And the Law does not say who may or may not pay that price. Am I right?"

"Good! good!" said the young wolves, who are always hungry. "Listen to Bagheera. The cub can be bought for a price. It is the Law."

"Knowing that I have no right to speak here, I ask your leave."

"Speak then," cried twenty voices.

"To kill a naked cub is shame. Besides, he may make better sport for you when he is grown. Baloo has spoken in his behalf. Now to Baloo's word I will add one bull, and a fat one, newly killed, not half a mile from here, if ye will accept the man's cub according to the Law. Is it difficult?"

There was a clamor of scores of voices, saying: "What matter? He will die in the winter rains. He will scorch in the sun. What harm can a naked frog do us? Let him run with the Pack. Where is the bull, Bagheera? Let him be accepted." And then came Akela's deep bay, crying: "Look well—look well, O Wolves!"

Mowgli was still playing with the pebbles, and he did not notice when the wolves came and looked at him one by one. At last they all went down the hill for the dead bull, and only Akela, Bagheera, Baloo, and Mowgli's own wolves were left. Shere Khan roared still in the night, for he was very angry that Mowgli had not been handed over to him.

"Ay, roar well," said Bagheera, under his whiskers; "for the time comes when this naked thing will make thee roar to another tune, or I know nothing of Man."

"It was well done," said Akela. "Men and their cubs are very wise. He may be a help in time."

"Truly, a help in time of need; for none can hope to lead the Pack forever," said Bagheera.

Akela said nothing. He was thinking of the

time that comes to every leader of every pack when his strength goes from him and he gets feebler and feebler, till at last he is killed by the wolves and a new leader comes up—to be killed in his turn.

"Take him away," he said to Father Wolf, "and train him as befits one of the Free People."

And that is how Mowgli was entered into the Seeonee wolf-pack for the price of a bull and on Baloo's good word.

Now you must be content to skip ten or eleven whole years, and only guess at all the wonderful life that Mowgli led among the wolves, because if it were written out it would fill ever so many books. He grew up with the cubs, though they of course were grown wolves almost before he was a child, and Father Wolf taught him his business, and the meaning of things in the jungle, till every rustle in the grass, every breath of the warm night air, every note of the owls above his head, every scratch of a bat's claws as it roosted for a while in a tree, and every splash of every little fish jumping in a pool, meant just as much to him as the work of his office means to a business man. When he was not learning he sat out in the sun and slept, and ate, and went to sleep again; when he felt

dirty or hot he swam in the forest pools; and
when he wanted honey (Baloo told him that
honey and nuts were just as pleasant to eat as
raw meat) he climbed up for it, and that
Bagheera showed him how to do.

Bagheera would lie out on a branch and
call, "Come along, Little Brother," and at first
Mowgli would cling like the sloth, but afterward he would fling himself through the
branches almost as boldly as the gray ape. He
took his place at the Council Rock, too, when
the Pack met, and there he discovered that if
he stared hard at any wolf, the wolf would be
forced to drop his eyes, and so he used to
stare for fun.

At other times he would pick the long
thorns out of the pads of his friends, for
wolves suffer terribly from thorns and burs in
their coats. He would go down the hillside
into the cultivated lands by night, and look
very curiously at the villagers in their huts,
but he had a mistrust of men because
Bagheera showed him a square box with a
drop-gate so cunningly hidden in the jungle
that he nearly walked into it, and told him it
was a trap.

He loved better than anything else to go
with Bagheera into the dark warm heart of
the forest, to sleep all through the drowsy

day, and at night see how Bagheera did his killing. Bagheera killed right and left as he felt hungry, and so did Mowgli—with one exception. As soon as he was old enough to understand things, Bagheera told him that he must never touch cattle because he had been bought into the Pack at the price of a bull's life. "All the jungle is thine," said Bagheera, "and thou canst kill everything that thou art strong enough to kill; but for the sake of the bull that bought thee thou must never kill or eat any cattle young or old. That is the Law of the Jungle." Mowgli obeyed faithfully.

And he grew and grew strong as a boy must grow who does not know that he is learning any lessons, and who has nothing in the world to think of except things to eat.

Mother Wolf told him once or twice that Shere Khan was not a creature to be trusted, and that some day he must kill Shere Khan; but though a young wolf would have remembered that advice every hour, Mowgli forgot it because he was only a boy—though he would have called himself a wolf if he had been able to speak in any human tongue.

Shere Khan was always crossing his path in the jungle, for as Akela grew older and feebler the lame tiger had come to be great friends with the younger wolves of the Pack, who fol-

lowed him for scraps, a thing Akela would
never have allowed if he had dared to push
his authority to the proper bounds. Then
Shere Khan would flatter them and wonder
that such fine young hunters were content
to be led by a dying wolf and a man's cub.
"They tell me," Shere Khan would say, "that at
Council ye dare not look him between the
eyes"; and the young wolves would growl and
bristle.

Bagheera, who had eyes and ears everywhere, knew something of this, and once or
twice he told Mowgli in so many words that
Shere Khan would kill him some day; and
Mowgli would laugh and answer: "I have the
Pack and I have thee; and Baloo, though he is
so lazy, might strike a blow or two for my
sake. Why should I be afraid?"

It was one very warm day that a new notion
came to Bagheera—born of something that he
had heard. Perhaps Ikki, the Porcupine, had
told him; but he said to Mowgli when they
were deep in the jungle, as the boy lay with
his head on Bagheera's beautiful black skin:
"Little Brother, how often have I told thee that
Shere Khan is thy enemy?"

"As many times as there are nuts on that
palm," said Mowgli, who, naturally, could not
count. "What of it? I am sleepy, Bagheera, and

Shere Khan is all long tail and loud talk, like Mao, the Peacock."

"But this is no time for sleeping. Baloo knows it, I know it, the Pack know it, and even the foolish, foolish deer know. Tabaqui has told thee too."

"Ho! ho!" said Mowgli. "Tabaqui came to me not long ago with some rude talk that I was a naked man's cub, and not fit to dig pig-nuts; but I caught Tabaqui by the tail and swung him twice against a palm-tree to teach him better manners."

"That was foolishness; for though Tabaqui is a mischief-maker, he would have told thee of something that concerned thee closely. Open those eyes, Little Brother! Shere Khan dares not kill thee in the jungle for fear of those that love thee; but remember, Akela is very old, and soon the day comes when he cannot kill his buck, and then he will be leader no more. Many of the wolves that looked thee over when thou wast brought to the Council first are old too, and the young wolves believe, as Shere Khan has taught them, that a man-cub has no place with the Pack. In a little time thou wilt be a man."

"And what is a man that he should not run with his brothers?" said Mowgli. "I was born in the jungle; I have obeyed the Law of the

Jungle; and there is no wolf of ours from whose paws I have not pulled a thorn. Surely they are my brothers!"

Bagheera stretched himself at full length and half shut his eyes. "Little Brother," said he, "feel under my jaw."

Mowgli put up his strong brown hand, and just under Bagheera's silky chin, where the giant rolling muscles were all hid by the glossy hair, he came upon a little bald spot.

"There is no one in the jungle that knows that I, Bagheera, carry that mark—the mark of the collar; and yet, Little Brother, I was born among men, and it was among men that my mother died—in the cages of the King's Palace at Oodeypore. It was because of this that I paid the price for thee at the Council when thou wast a little naked cub. Yes, I too was born among men. I had never seen the jungle. They fed me behind bars from an iron pan till one night I felt that I was Bagheera, the Panther, and no man's plaything, and I broke the silly lock with one blow of my paw, and came away; and because I had learned the ways of men, I became more terrible in the jungle than Shere Khan. Is it not so?"

"Yes," said Mowgli; "all the jungle fear Bagheera—all except Mowgli."

"Oh, *thou* art a man's cub," said the Black

Panther, very tenderly; "and even as I returned to my jungle, so thou must go back to men at last,—to the men who are thy brothers,—if thou art not killed in the Council."

"But why—but why should any wish to kill me?" said Mowgli.

"Look at me," said Bagheera; and Mowgli looked at him steadily between the eyes. The big panther turned his head away in half a minute.

"*That* is why," he said, shifting his paw on the leaves. "Not even I can look thee between the eyes, and I was born among men, and I love thee, Little Brother. The others they hate thee because their eyes cannot meet thine; because thou art wise; because thou hast pulled out thorns from their feet—because thou art a man."

"I did not know these things," said Mowgli, sullenly; and he frowned under his heavy black eyebrows.

"What is the Law of the Jungle? Strike first and then give tongue. By thy very carelessness they know that thou art a man. But be wise. It is in my heart that when Akela misses his next kill,—and at each hunt it costs him more to pin the buck,—the Pack will turn against him and against thee. They will hold a jungle Council at the Rock, and then—and then . . . I have it!" said Bagheera, leaping up. "Go thou down quickly to the men's huts in the valley, and take some of the Red Flower which they grow there, so that when the time comes thou mayest have even a stronger friend than I or Baloo or those of the Pack that love thee. Get the Red Flower."

By Red Flower Bagheera meant fire, only no creature in the jungle will call fire by its proper name. Every beast lives in deadly fear of it, and invents a hundred ways of describing it.

"The Red Flower?" said Mowgli. "That grows outside their huts in the twilight. I will get some."

"There speaks the man's cub," said Bagheera, proudly. "Remember that it grows in little pots. Get one swiftly, and keep it by thee for time of need."

"Good!" said Mowgli. "I go. But art thou sure, O my Bagheera"—he slipped his arm round the splendid neck, and looked deep into the big eyes—"art thou sure that all this is Shere Khan's doing?"

"By the Broken Lock that freed me, I am sure, Little Brother."

"Then, by the Bull that bought me, I will pay Shere Khan full tale for this, and it may be a little over," said Mowgli; and he bounded away.

"That is a man. That is all a man," said Bagheera to himself, lying down again. "Oh, Shere Khan, never was a blacker hunting than that frog-hunt of thine ten years ago!"

Mowgli was far and far through the forest, running hard, and his heart was hot in him. He came to the cave as the evening mist rose, and drew breath, and looked down the valley. The cubs were out, but Mother Wolf, at the back of the cave, knew by his breathing that something was troubling her frog.

"What is it, Son?" she said.

"Some bat's chatter of Shere Khan," he called back. "I hunt among the plowed fields to-night"; and he plunged downward through the bushes, to the stream at the bottom of the valley. There he checked, for he heard the yell of the Pack hunting, heard the bellow of a hunted Sambhur, and the snort as the buck turned at bay. Then there were wicked, bitter howls from the young wolves: "Akela! Akela! Let the Lone Wolf show his strength. Room for the leader of our Pack! Spring, Akela!"

The Lone Wolf must have sprung and missed his hold, for Mowgli heard the snap of his teeth and then a yelp as the Sambhur knocked him over with his fore foot.

He did not wait for anything more, but

dashed on; and the yells grew fainter behind him as he ran into the crop-lands where the villagers lived.

"Bagheera spoke truth," he panted, as he nestled down in some cattle-fodder by the window of a hut. "To-morrow is one day for Akela and for me."

Then he pressed his face close to the window and watched the fire on the hearth. He saw the husbandman's wife get up and feed it in the night with black lumps; and when the morning came and the mists were all white and cold, he saw the man's child pick up a wicker pot plastered inside with earth, fill it with lumps of red-hot charcoal, put it under his blanket, and go out to tend the cows in the byre.

"Is that all?" said Mowgli. "If a cub can do it, there is nothing to fear"; so he strode around the corner and met the boy, took the pot from his hand, and disappeared into the mist while the boy howled with fear.

"They are very like me," said Mowgli, blowing into the pot, as he had seen the woman do. "This thing will die if I do not give it things to eat"; and he dropped twigs and dried bark on the red stuff. Half-way up the hill he met Bagheera with the morning dew shining like moonstones on his coat.

"Akela has missed," said the panther. "They

would have killed him last night, but they needed thee also. They were looking for thee on the hill."

"I was among the plowed lands. I am ready. Look!" Mowgli held up the fire-pot.

"Good! Now, I have seen men thrust a dry branch into that stuff, and presently the Red Flower blossomed at the end of it. Art thou not afraid?"

"No. Why should I fear? I remember now— if it is not a dream—how, before I was a wolf, I lay beside the Red Flower, and it was warm and pleasant."

All that day Mowgli sat in the cave tending his fire-pot and dipping dry branches into it to see how they looked. He found a branch that satisfied him, and in the evening when Tabaqui came to the cave and told him, rudely enough, that he was wanted at the Council Rock, he laughed till Tabaqui ran away. Then Mowgli went to the Council, still laughing.

Akela the Lone Wolf lay by the side of his rock as a sign that the leadership of the Pack was open, and Shere Khan with his following of scrap-fed wolves walked to and fro openly, being flattered. Bagheera lay close to Mowgli, and the fire-pot was between Mowgli's knees. When they were all gathered together, Shere Khan began to speak—a thing he would never have dared to do when Akela was in his prime.

"He has no right," whispered Bagheera. "Say so. He is a dog's son. He will be frightened."

Mowgli sprang to his feet. "Free People," he cried, "does Shere Khan lead the Pack? What has a tiger to do with our leadership?"

"Seeing that the leadership is yet open, and being asked to speak"—Shere Khan began.

"By whom?" said Mowgli. "Are we *all* jackals, to fawn on this cattle-butcher? The leadership of the Pack is with the Pack alone."

There were yells of "Silence, thou man's cub!" "Let him speak; he has kept our law!" And at last the seniors of the Pack thundered: "Let the Dead Wolf speak!"

When a leader of the Pack has missed his kill, he is called the Dead Wolf as long as he lives, which is not long, as a rule.

Akela raised his old head wearily:

"Free people, and ye too, jackals of Shere Khan, for twelve seasons I have led ye to and from the kill, and in all that time not one has been trapped or maimed. Now I have missed my kill. Ye know how that plot was made. Ye know how ye brought me up to an untried buck to make my weakness known. It was cleverly done. Your right is to kill me here on the Council Rock now. Therefore I ask, 'Who comes to make an end of the Lone Wolf?' For it is my right, by the Law of the Jungle, that ye come one by one."

There was a long hush, for no single wolf cared to fight Akela to the death. Then Shere Khan roared: "Bah! What have we to do with this toothless fool? He is doomed to die! It is the man-cub who has lived too long. Free People, he was my meat from the first. Give him to me. I am weary of this man-wolf folly. He has troubled the jungle for ten seasons. Give me the man-cub, or I will hunt here always, and not give you one bone! He is a man—a man's child, and from the marrow of my bones I hate him!"

Then more than half the Pack yelled: "A man—a man! What has a man to do with us? Let him go to his own place."

"And turn all the people of the villages against us?" snarled Shere Khan. "No; give him to me. He is a man, and none of us can look him between the eyes."

Akela lifted his head again, and said: "He has eaten our food; he has slept with us; he has driven game for us; he has broken no word of the Law of the Jungle."

"Also, I paid for him with a bull when he was accepted. The worth of a bull is little, but Bagheera's honor is something that he will perhaps fight for," said Bagheera in his gentlest voice.

"A bull paid ten years ago!" the Pack snarled. "What do we care for bones ten years old?"

"Or for a pledge?" said Bagheera, his white teeth bared under his lip. "Well are ye called the Free People!"

"No man's cub can run with the people of the jungle!" roared Shere Khan. "Give him to me."

"He is our brother in all but blood," Akela went on; "and ye would kill him here. In truth, I have lived too long. Some of ye are eaters of cattle, and of others I have heard that, under Shere Khan's teaching, ye go by dark night and snatch children from the villager's doorstep. Therefore I know ye to be cowards, and it is to cowards I speak. It is certain that I must die, and my life is of no worth, or I would offer that in the man-cub's place. But for the sake of the Honor of the Pack,—a little matter that, by being without a leader, ye have forgotten,—I promise that if ye let the man-cub go to his own place, I will not, when my time comes to die, bare one tooth against ye. I will die without fighting. That will at least save the Pack three lives. More I cannot do; but, if ye will, I can save ye the shame that comes of killing a brother against whom there is no fault—a brother spoken for and bought into the Pack according to the Law of the Jungle."

"He is a man—a man—a man!" snarled the Pack; and most of the wolves began to gather round Shere Khan, whose tail was beginning to switch.

"Now the business is in thy hands," said Bagheera to Mowgli. "*We* can do no more except fight."

Mowgli stood upright—the fire-pot in his hands. Then he stretched out his arms, and yawned in the face of the Council; but he was furious with rage and sorrow, for, wolf-like, the wolves had never told him how they hated him.

"Listen, you!" he cried. "There is no need for this dog's jabber. Ye have told me so often to-night that I am a man (though indeed I would have been a wolf with you to my life's end) that I feel your words are true. So I do not call ye my brothers any more, but *sag* [dogs], as a man should. What ye will do, and what ye will not do, is not yours to say. That matter is with *me;* and that we may see the matter more plainly, I, the man, have brought here a little of the Red Flower which ye, dogs, fear."

He flung the fire-pot on the ground, and some of the red coals lit a tuft of dried moss that flared up as all the Council drew back in terror before the leaping flames.

Mowgli thrust his dead branch into the fire till the twigs lit and crackled, and whirled it above his head among the cowering wolves.

"Thou art the master," said Bagheera, in an undertone. "Save Akela from the death. He was ever thy friend."

Akela, the grim old wolf who had never asked for mercy in his life, gave one piteous look at Mowgli as the boy stood all naked, his long black hair tossing over his shoulders in the light of the blazing branch that made the shadows jump and quiver.

"Good!" said Mowgli, staring around slowly, and thrusting out his lower lip. "I see that ye are dogs. I go from you to my own people—if they be my own people. The jungle is shut to me, and I must forget your talk and your companionship; but I will be more merciful than ye are. Because I was all but your brother in blood, I promise that when I am a man among men I will not betray ye to men as ye have betrayed me." He kicked the fire with his foot, and the sparks flew up. "There shall be no war between any of us and the Pack. But here is a debt to pay before I go." He strode forward to

"Up, when a man speaks, or I will set that coat ablaze!"

where Shere Khan sat blinking stupidly at the flames, and caught him by the tuft on his chin. Bagheera followed close, in case of accidents. "Up, dog!" Mowgli cried. "Up, when a man speaks, or I will set that coat ablaze!"

Shere Khan's ears lay flat back on his head, and he shut his eyes, for the blazing branch was very near.

"This cattle-killer said he would kill me in the Council because he had not killed me when I was a cub. Thus and thus, then, do we beat dogs when we are men! Stir a whisker, Lungri, and I ram the Red Flower down thy gullet!" He beat Shere Khan over the head with the branch, and the tiger whimpered and whined in an agony of fear.

"Pah! Singed jungle-cat—go now! But remember when next I come to the Council Rock, as a man should come, it will be with Shere Khan's hide on my head. For the rest, Akela goes free to live as he pleases. Ye will *not* kill him, because that is not my will. Nor do I think that ye will sit here any longer, lolling out your tongues as though ye were somebodies, instead of dogs whom I drive out— thus! Go!"

The fire was burning furiously at the end of the branch, and Mowgli struck right and left round the circle, and the wolves ran howling with the sparks burning their fur. At last there were only Akela, Bagheera, and perhaps ten wolves that had taken Mowgli's part. Then something began to hurt Mowgli inside him, as he had never been hurt in his life before, and he caught his breath and sobbed, and the tears ran down his face.

"What is it? What is it?" he said. "I do not wish to leave the jungle, and I do not know what this is. Am I dying, Bagheera?"

"No, Little Brother. Those are only tears such as men use," said Bagheera. "Now I know thou art a man, and a man's cub no longer. The jungle is shut indeed to thee henceforward. Let them fall, Mowgli; they are only tears." So Mowgli sat and cried as though his heart would break; and he had never cried in all his life before.

"Now," he said, "I will go to men. But first I must say farewell to my mother"; and he went to the cave where she lived with Father Wolf, and he cried on her coat, while the four cubs howled miserably.

"Ye will not forget me?" said Mowgli.

"Never while we can follow a trail," said the cubs. "Come to the foot of the hill when thou art a man, and we will talk to thee; and we will come into the crop-lands to play with thee by night."

"Come soon!" said Father Wolf. "Oh, wise little Frog, come again soon; for we be old, thy mother and I."

"Come soon," said Mother Wolf, "little naked son of mine; for, listen, child of man, I loved thee more than ever I loved my cubs."

"I will surely come," said Mowgli; "and when I come it will be to lay out Shere Khan's hide upon the Council Rock. Do not forget me! Tell them in the jungle never to forget me!"

The dawn was beginning to break when Mowgli went down the hillside alone to the crops to meet those mysterious things that are called men.

HUNTING-SONG OF
THE SEEONEE PACK

As the dawn was breaking the Sambhur
   belled
     Once, twice, and again!
And a doe leaped up—and a doe leaped up
From the pond in the wood where the wild
   deer sup.
This I, scouting alone, beheld,
     Once, twice, and again!

As the dawn was breaking the Sambhur
   belled
     Once, twice, and again!

And a wolf stole back—and a wolf stole back
To carry the word to the waiting Pack;
And we sought and we found and we bayed
    on his track
        Once, twice, and again!

As the dawn was breaking the Wolf-pack
    yelled
        Once, twice, and again!
Feet in the jungle that leave no mark!
Eyes that can see in the dark—the dark!
Tongue—give tongue to it! Hark! O Hark!
        Once, twice, and again!

Kaa's Hunting

His spots are the joy of the Leopard: his horns are
    the Buffalo's pride—
Be clean, for the strength of the hunter is known
    by the gloss of his hide.

If ye find that the Bullock can toss you, or the
    heavy-browed Sambhur can gore;
Ye need not stop work to inform us; we knew it
    ten seasons before.

Oppress not the cubs of the stranger, but hail
    them as Sister and Brother,
For though they are little and fubsy, it may be the
    Bear is their mother.

"There is none like to me!" says the Cub in the
    pride of his earliest kill;
But the Jungle is large and the Cub he is small. Let
    him think and be still.

Maxims of Baloo.

Kaa's Hunting

ALL THAT IS TOLD here happened some time before Mowgli was turned out of the Seeonee wolf-pack. It was in the days when Baloo was teaching him the Law of the Jungle. The big, serious, old brown bear was delighted to have so quick a pupil, for the young wolves will only learn as much of the Law of the Jungle as applies to their own pack and tribe, and run away as soon as they can repeat the Hunting Verse: "Feet that make no noise; eyes that can see in the dark; ears that can hear the winds in their lairs, and sharp white teeth—all these things are the marks of our brothers except Tabaqui and the Hyena, whom we hate." But Mowgli, as a man-cub, had to learn a great deal more than this. Sometimes Bagheera, the Black Panther, would come lounging through the jungle to see how his pet was getting on, and would purr with his head against a tree while Mowgli recited the day's lesson to Baloo. The boy

41

could climb almost as well as he could swim,
and swim almost as well as he could run; so
Baloo, the Teacher of the Law, taught him the
Wood and Water laws: how to tell a rotten
branch from a sound one; how to speak
politely to the wild bees when he came upon a
hive of them fifty feet aboveground; what to
say to Mang, the Bat, when he disturbed him
in the branches at midday; and how to warn
the water-snakes in the pools before he
splashed down among them. None of the Jungle People like being disturbed, and all are
very ready to fly at an intruder. Then, too,
Mowgli was taught the Strangers' Hunting
Call, which must be repeated aloud till it is
answered, whenever one of the Jungle People
hunts outside his own grounds. It means,
translated: "Give me leave to hunt here
because I am hungry"; and the answer is:
"Hunt, then, for food, but not for pleasure."

All this will show you how much Mowgli
had to learn by heart, and he grew very tired
of repeating the same thing a hundred times;
but, as Baloo said to Bagheera one day when
Mowgli had been cuffed and had run off in a
temper: "A man's cub is a man's cub, and he
must learn *all* the Law of the Jungle."

"But think how small he is," said the Black
Panther, who would have spoiled Mowgli if he

had had his own way. "How can his little head carry all thy long talk?"

"Is there anything in the jungle too little to be killed? No. That is why I teach him these things, and that is why I hit him, very softly, when he forgets."

"Softly! What dost thou know of softness, old Iron-feet?" Bagheera grunted. "His face is all bruised to-day by thy—softness. Ugh!"

"Better he should be bruised from head to foot by me who love him than that he should come to harm through ignorance," Baloo answered, very earnestly. "I am now teaching him the Master Words of the Jungle that shall protect him with the Birds and the Snake People, and all that hunt on four feet, except his own pack. He can now claim protection, if he will only remember the Words, from all in the jungle. Is not that worth a little beating?"

"Well, look to it then that thou dost not kill the man-cub. He is no tree-trunk to sharpen thy blunt claws upon. But what are those Master Words? I am more likely to give help than to ask it"—Bagheera stretched out one paw and admired the steel-blue ripping-chisel talons at the end of it—"Still I should like to know."

"I will call Mowgli and he shall say them—if he will. Come, Little Brother!"

"My head is ringing like a bee-tree," said a sullen voice over their heads, and Mowgli slid down a tree-trunk, very angry and indignant, adding, as he reached the ground: "I come for Bagheera and not for *thee*, fat old Baloo!"

"That is all one to me," said Baloo, though he was hurt and grieved. "Tell Bagheera, then, the Master Words of the Jungle that I have taught thee this day."

"Master Words for which people?" said Mowgli, delighted to show off. "The jungle has many tongues. *I* know them all."

"A little thou knowest, but not much. See, O Bagheera, they never thank their teacher! Not one small wolfling has come back to thank old Baloo for his teachings. Say the Word for the Hunting People, then,—great scholar!"

"We be of one blood, ye and I," said Mowgli, giving the words the Bear accent which all the Hunting People of the Jungle use.

"Good! Now for the Birds."

Mowgli repeated, with the Kite's whistle at the end of the sentence.

"Now for the Snake People," said Bagheera.

The answer was a perfectly indescribable hiss, and Mowgli kicked up his feet behind, clapped his hands together to applaud himself, and jumped on Bagheera's back, where he sat sideways, drumming with his heels on the glossy skin and making the worst faces that he could think of at Baloo.

"There—there! That was worth a little bruise," said the Brown Bear, tenderly. "Some day thou wilt remember me." Then he turned aside to tell Bagheera how he had begged the Master Words from Hathi, the Wild Elephant, who knows all about these things, and how Hathi had taken Mowgli down to a pool to get the Snake Word from a water-snake, because Baloo could not pronounce it, and how Mowgli was now reasonably safe against all accidents in the jungle, because neither snake, bird, nor beast would hurt him.

"No one then is to be feared," Baloo wound up, patting his big furry stomach with pride.

"Except his own tribe," said Bagheera, under his breath; and then aloud to Mowgli: "Have a care for my ribs, Little Brother! What is all this dancing up and down?"

Mowgli had been trying to make himself heard by pulling at Bagheera's shoulder-fur and kicking hard. When the two listened to him he was shouting at the top of his voice: "And *so* I shall have a tribe of my own, and lead them through the branches all day long."

"What is this new folly, little dreamer of dreams?" said Bagheera.

"Yes, and throw branches and dirt at old

Baloo," Mowgli went on. "They have promised me this, ah!"

"Whoof!" Baloo's big paw scooped Mowgli off Bagheera's back, and as the boy lay between the big fore paws he could see the bear was angry.

"Mowgli," said Baloo, "thou hast been talking with the Bandar-log—the Monkey People."

Mowgli looked at Bagheera to see if the panther was angry too, and Bagheera's eyes were as hard as jade-stones.

"Thou hast been with the Monkey People— the gray apes—the people without a Law—the eaters of everything. That is great shame."

"When Baloo hurt my head," said Mowgli (he was still down on his back), "I went away, and the gray apes came down from the trees and had pity on me. No one else cared." He snuffled a little.

"The pity of the Monkey People!" Baloo snorted.

"The stillness of the mountain stream! The cool of the summer sun! And then, man-cub?"

"And then—and then they gave me nuts and pleasant things to eat, and they—they carried me in their arms up to the top of the trees and said I was their blood-brother, except that I had no tail, and should be their leader some day."

"They have *no* leader," said Bagheera. "They lie. They have always lied."

"They were very kind, and bade me come again. Why have I never been taken among the Monkey People? They stand on their feet as I do. They do not hit me with hard paws. They play all day. Let me get up! Bad Baloo, let me up! I will go play with them again."

"Listen, man-cub," said the bear, and his ·voice rumbled like thunder on a hot night. "I have taught thee all the Law of the Jungle for all the Peoples of the Jungle—except the Monkey Folk who live in the trees. They have no Law. They are outcastes. They have no speech of their own, but use the stolen words which they overhear when they listen and peep and wait up above in the branches. Their way is not our way. They are without leaders. They have no remembrance. They boast and chatter and pretend that they are a great people about to do great affairs in the jungle, but the falling of a nut turns their minds to laughter, and all is forgotten. We of the jungle have no dealings with them. We do not drink where the monkeys drink; we do not go where the monkeys go; we do not hunt where they hunt; we do not die where they die. Hast thou ever heard me speak of the Bandar-log till to-day?"

"No," said Mowgli in a whisper, for the forest was very still now that Baloo had finished.

"The Jungle People put them out of their mouths and out of their minds. They are very many, evil, dirty, shameless, and they desire, if they have any fixed desire, to be noticed by the Jungle People. But we do *not* notice them even when they throw nuts and filth on our heads."

He had hardly spoken when a shower of nuts and twigs spattered down through the branches; and they could hear coughings and howlings and angry jumpings high up in the air among the thin branches.

"The Monkey People are forbidden," said Baloo, "forbidden to the Jungle People. Remember."

"Forbidden," said Bagheera; "but I still think Baloo should have warned thee against them."

"I—I? How was I to guess he would play with such dirt. The Monkey People! Faugh!"

A fresh shower came down on their heads, and the two trotted away, taking Mowgli with them. What Baloo had said about the monkeys was perfectly true. They belonged to the tree-tops, and as beasts very seldom look up, there was no occasion for the monkeys and the Jungle People to cross one another's path.

But whenever they found a sick wolf, or a wounded tiger or bear, the monkeys would torment him, and would throw sticks and nuts at any beast for fun and in the hope of being noticed. Then they would howl and shriek senseless songs, and invite the Jungle People to climb up their trees and fight them, or would start furious battles over nothing among themselves, and leave the dead monkeys where the Jungle People could see them.

They were always just going to have a leader and laws and customs of their own, but they never did, because their memories would not hold over from day to day, and so they settled things by making up a saying: "What the Bandar-log think now the Jungle will think later"; and that comforted them a great deal. None of the beasts could reach them, but on the other hand none of the beasts would notice them, and that was why they were so pleased when Mowgli came to play with them, and when they heard how angry Baloo was.

They never meant to do any more,—the Bandar-log never mean anything at all,—but one of them invented what seemed to him a brilliant idea, and he told all the others that Mowgli would be a useful person to keep in the tribe, because he could weave sticks together for protection from the wind; so, if they caught him, they could make him teach them. Of course Mowgli, as a wood-cutter's child, inherited all sorts of instincts, and used to make little play-huts of fallen branches without thinking how he came to do it. The Monkey People, watching in the trees, considered these huts most wonderful. This time, they said, they were really going to have a leader and become the wisest people in the jungle—so wise that every one else would notice and envy them. Therefore they followed Baloo and Bagheera and Mowgli through the jungle very quietly till it was time for the midday nap, and Mowgli, who was very much ashamed of himself, slept between the panther and the bear, resolving to have no more to do with the Monkey People.

The next thing he remembered was feeling hands on his legs and arms,—hard, strong little hands,—and then a swash of branches in his face; and then he was staring down through the swaying boughs as Baloo woke the jungle with his deep cries and Bagheera bounded up the trunk with every tooth bared. The Bandar-log howled with triumph, and scuffled away to the upper branches where Bagheera dared not follow, shouting: "He has noticed us! Bagheera has noticed us! All the Jungle People admire us for our skill and our

The next thing he remembered was feeling hands on his legs and arms—and then a swash of branches in his face.

cunning!" Then they began their flight; and the
flight of the Monkey People through tree-land
is one of the things nobody can describe.
They have their regular roads and cross-
roads, uphills and downhills, all laid out from
fifty to seventy or a hundred feet aboveground, and by these they can travel even at
night if necessary.

Two of the strongest monkeys caught
Mowgli under the arms and swung off with
him through the tree-tops, twenty feet at a
bound. Had they been alone they could have
gone twice as fast, but the boy's weight held
them back. Sick and giddy as Mowgli was he
could not help enjoying the wild rush, though
the glimpses of earth far down below frightened him, and the terrible check and jerk at
the end of the swing over nothing but empty
air brought his heart between his teeth.

His escort would rush him up a tree till he
felt the weak topmost branches crackle and
bend under them, and, then, with a cough and
a whoop, would fling themselves into the air
outward and downward, and bring up hanging
by their hands or their feet to the lower limbs
of the next tree. Sometimes he could see for
miles and miles over the still green jungle, as
a man on the top of a mast can see for miles
across the sea, and then the branches and

leaves would lash him across the face, and he and his two guards would be almost down to earth again.

So bounding and crashing and whooping and yelling, the whole tribe of Bandar-log swept along the tree-roads with Mowgli their prisoner.

For a time he was afraid of being dropped; then he grew angry, but he knew better than to struggle; and then he began to think. The first thing was to send back word to Baloo and Bagheera, for, at the pace the monkeys were going, he knew his friends would be left far behind. It was useless to look down, for he could see only the top-sides of the branches, so he stared upward and saw, far away in the blue, Rann, the Kite, balancing and wheeling as he kept watch over the jungle waiting for things to die. Rann noticed that the monkeys were carrying something, and dropped a few hundred yards to find out whether their load was good to eat. He whistled with surprise when he saw Mowgli being dragged up to a tree-top, and heard him give the Kite call for "We be of one blood, thou and I." The waves of the branches closed over the boy, but Rann balanced away to the next tree in time to see the little brown face come up again. "Mark my trail!" Mowgli shouted. "Tell Baloo of the

Seeonee Pack, and Bagheera of the Council Rock."

"In whose name, Brother?" Rann had never seen Mowgli before, though of course he had heard of him.

"Mowgli, the Frog. Man-cub they call me! Mark my tra—il!"

The last words were shrieked as he was being swung through the air, but Rann nodded, and rose up till he looked no bigger than a speck of dust, and there he hung, watching with his telescope eyes the swaying of the tree-tops as Mowgli's escort whirled along.

"They never go far," he said, with a chuckle. "They never do what they set out to do. Always pecking at new things are the Bandar-log. This time, if I have any eyesight, they have pecked down trouble for themselves, for Baloo is no fledgling and Bagheera can, as I know, kill more than goats."

Then he rocked on his wings, his feet gathered up under him, and waited.

Meanwhile, Baloo and Bagheera were furious with rage and grief. Bagheera climbed as he had never climbed before, but the branches broke beneath his weight, and he slipped down, his claws full of bark.

"Why didst thou not warn the man-cub!" he roared to poor Baloo, who had set off at a clumsy trot in the hope of overtaking the monkeys. "What was the use of half slaying him with blows if thou didst not warn him?"

"Haste! O haste! We—we may catch them yet!" Baloo panted.

"At that speed! It would not tire a wounded cow. Teacher of the Law, cub-beater—a mile of that rolling to and fro would burst thee open. Sit still and think! Make a plan. This is no time for chasing. They may drop him if we follow too close."

"*Arrula! Whoo!* They may have dropped him already, being tired of carrying him. Who can trust the Bandar-log? Put dead bats on my head! Give me black bones to eat! Roll me into the hives of the wild bees that I may be stung to death, and bury me with the hyena; for I am the most miserable of bears! *Arulala! Wahooa!* O Mowgli, Mowgli! Why did I not warn thee against the Monkey Folk instead of breaking thy head? Now perhaps I may have knocked the day's lesson out of his mind, and he will be alone in the jungle without the Master Words!"

Baloo clasped his paws over his ears and rolled to and fro, moaning.

"At least he gave me all the Words correctly a little time ago," said Bagheera, impatiently. "Baloo, thou hast neither memory nor respect.

What would the jungle think if I, the Black Panther, curled myself up like Ikki, the Porcupine, and howled?"

"What do I care what the jungle thinks? He may be dead by now."

"Unless and until they drop him from the branches in sport, or kill him out of idleness, I have no fear for the man-cub. He is wise and well-taught, and, above all, he has the eyes that make the Jungle People afraid. But (and it is a great evil) he is in the power of the Bandar-log, and they, because they live in trees, have no fear of any of our people." Bagheera licked his one fore paw thoughtfully.

"Fool that I am! Oh fat, brown, root-digging fool that I am!" said Baloo, uncoiling himself with a jerk. "It is true what Hathi, the Wild Elephant, says: *'To each his own fear'*; and they, the Bandar-log, fear Kaa, the Rock Snake. He can climb as well as they can. He steals the young monkeys in the night. The mere whisper of his name makes their wicked tails cold. Let us go to Kaa."

"What will he do for us? He is not of our tribe, being footless and with most evil eyes," said Bagheera.

"He is very old and very cunning. Above all, he is always hungry," said Baloo, hopefully. "Promise him many goats."

"He sleeps for a full month after he has once eaten. He may be asleep now, and even were he awake, what if he would rather kill his own goats?" Bagheera, who did not know much about Kaa, was naturally suspicious.

"Then in that case, thou and I together, old hunter, may make him see reason." Here Baloo rubbed his faded brown shoulder against the panther, and they went off to look for Kaa, the Rock Python.

They found him stretched out on a warm ledge in the afternoon sun, admiring his beautiful new coat, for he had been in retirement for the last ten days changing his skin, and now he was very splendid—darting his big blunt-nosed head along the ground, and twisting the thirty feet of his body into fantastic knots and curves, and licking his lips as he thought of his dinner to come.

"He has not eaten," said Baloo, with a grunt of relief, as soon as he saw the beautifully mottled brown and yellow jacket. "Be careful, Bagheera! He is always a little blind after he has changed his skin, and very quick to strike."

Kaa was not a poison snake—in fact he rather despised the Poison Snakes for cowards; but his strength lay in his hug, and when he had once lapped his huge coils round anybody there was no more to be said. "Good hunting!" cried Baloo, sitting up on his haunches. Like all snakes of his breed Kaa was rather deaf, and did not hear the call at first. Then he curled up ready for any accident, his head lowered.

"Good hunting for us all," he answered. "Oho, Baloo, what dost thou do here? Good hunting, Bagheera. One of us at least needs food. Is there any news of game afoot? A doe now, or even a young buck? I am as empty as a dried well."

"We are hunting," said Baloo, carelessly. He knew that you must not hurry Kaa. He is too big.

"Give me permission to come with you," said Kaa. "A blow more or less is nothing to thee, Bagheera or Baloo, but I—I have to wait and wait for days in a wood path and climb half a night on the mere chance of a young ape. *Pss naw!* The branches are not what they were when I was young. Rotten twigs and dry boughs are they all."

"Maybe thy great weight has something to do with the matter," said Baloo.

"I am a fair length—a fair length," said Kaa, with a little pride. "But for all that, it is the fault of this new-grown timber. I came very near to falling on my last hunt,—very near indeed,—and the noise of my slipping, for my tail was not tight wrapped round the tree, waked the Bandar-log, and they called me most evil names."

" 'Footless, yellow earthworm,' " said Bagheera under his whiskers, as though he were trying to remember something.

"*Sssss!* Have they ever called me *that?*" said Kaa.

"Something of that kind it was that they shouted to us last moon, but we never noticed them. They will say anything—even that thou hast lost all thy teeth, and dare not face anything bigger than a kid, because (they are indeed shameless, these Bandar-log)— because thou art afraid of the he-goats' horns," Bagheera went on sweetly.

Now a snake, especially a wary old python like Kaa, very seldom shows that he is angry; but Baloo and Bagheera could see the big swallowing muscles on either side of Kaa's throat ripple and bulge.

"The Bandar-log have shifted their grounds," he said, quietly. "When I came up into the sun to-day I heard them whooping among the tree-tops."

"It—it is the Bandar-log that we follow now," said Baloo; but the words stuck in his throat, for this was the first time in his memory that one of the Jungle People had owned to being interested in the doings of the monkeys.

"Beyond doubt, then, it is no small thing that takes two such hunters—leaders in their own jungle, I am certain—on the trail of the Bandar-log," Kaa replied, courteously, as he swelled with curiosity.

"Indeed," Baloo began, "I am no more than the old, and sometimes very foolish, Teacher of the Law to the Seeonee wolf-cubs, and Bagheera here—"

"Is Bagheera," said the Black Panther, and his jaws shut with a snap, for he did not believe in being humble. "The trouble is this, Kaa. Those nut-stealers and pickers of palm-leaves have stolen away our man-cub, of whom thou hast perhaps heard."

"I heard some news from Ikki (his quills make him presumptuous) of a man-thing that was entered into a wolf-pack, but I did not believe. Ikki is full of stories half heard and very badly told."

"But it is true. He is such a man-cub as never was," said Baloo. "The best and wisest and boldest of man-cubs. My own pupil, who shall make the name of Baloo famous through all the jungles; and besides, I—we—love him, Kaa."

"*Ts! Ts!*" said Kaa, shaking his head to and

fro. "I also have known what love is. There are tales I could tell that—"

"That need a clear night when we are all well fed to praise properly," said Bagheera, quickly. "Our man-cub is in the hands of the Bandar-log now, and we know that of all the Jungle People they fear Kaa alone."

"They fear me alone. They have good reason," said Kaa. "Chattering, foolish, vain—vain, foolish, and chattering—are the monkeys. But a man-thing in their hands is in no good luck. They grow tired of the nuts they pick, and throw them down. They carry a branch half a day, meaning to do great things with it, and then they snap it in two. That manling is not to be envied. They called me also—'yellow fish,' was it not?"

"Worm—worm—earthworm," said Bagheera; "as well as other things which I cannot now say for shame."

"We must remind them to speak well of their master. *Aaa-sssh!* We must help their wandering memories. Now, whither went they with thy cub?"

"The jungle alone knows. Toward the sunset, I believe," said Baloo. "We had thought that thou wouldst know, Kaa."

"I? How? I take them when they come in my way, but I do not hunt the Bandar-log—or frogs—or green scum on a water-hole, for that matter."

"Up, up! Up, up! *Hillo! Illo! Illo!* Look up, Baloo of the Seeonee Wolf Pack!"

Baloo looked up to see where the voice came from, and there was Rann, the Kite, sweeping down with the sun shining on the upturned flanges of his wings. It was near Rann's bedtime, but he had ranged all over the jungle looking for the bear, and missed him in the thick foliage.

"What is it?" said Baloo.

"I have seen Mowgli among the Bandar-log. He bade me tell you. I watched. The Bandar-log have taken him beyond the river to the Monkey City—to the Cold Lairs. They may stay there for a night, or ten nights, or an hour. I have told the bats to watch through the dark time. That is my message. Good hunting, all you below!"

"Full gorge and a deep sleep to you, Rann!" cried Bagheera. "I will remember thee in my next kill, and put aside the head for thee alone, O best of kites!"

"It is nothing. It is nothing. The boy held the Master Word. I could have done no less," and Rann circled up again to his roost.

"He has not forgotten to use his tongue," said Baloo, with a chuckle of pride. "To think

of one so young remembering the Master
Word for the birds while he was being pulled
across trees!"

"It was most firmly driven into him," said
Bagheera. "But I am proud of him, and now
we must go to the Cold Lairs."

They all knew where that place was, but
few of the Jungle People ever went there,
because what they called the Cold Lairs was
an old deserted city, lost and buried in the
jungle, and beasts seldom use a place that
men have once used. The wild boar will, but
the hunting-tribes do not. Besides, the monkeys lived there as much as they could be said
to live anywhere, and no self-respecting animal would come within eye-shot of it except
in times of drouth, when the half-ruined tanks
and reservoirs held a little water.

"It is half a night's journey—at full speed,"
said Bagheera. Baloo looked very serious. "I
will go as fast as I can," he said, anxiously.

"We dare not wait for thee. Follow, Baloo.
We must go on the quick-foot—Kaa and I."

"Feet or no feet, I can keep abreast of all
thy four," said Kaa, shortly.

Baloo made one effort to hurry, but had to
sit down panting, and so they left him to come
on later, while Bagheera hurried forward, at
the rocking panther-canter. Kaa said nothing,

but, strive as Bagheera might, the huge Rock Python held level with him. When they came to a hill-stream, Bagheera gained, because he bounded across while Kaa swam, his head and two feet of his neck clearing the water, but on level ground Kaa made up the distance.

"By the Broken Lock that freed me," said Bagheera, when twilight had fallen, "thou art no slow-goer."

"I am hungry," said Kaa. "Besides, they called me speckled frog."

"Worm—earthworm, and yellow to boot."

"All one. Let us go on," and Kaa seemed to pour himself along the ground, finding the shortest road with his steady eyes, and keeping to it.

In the Cold Lairs the Monkey People were not thinking of Mowgli's friends at all. They had brought the boy to the Lost City, and were very pleased with themselves for the time. Mowgli had never seen an Indian city before, and though this was almost a heap of ruins it seemed very wonderful and splendid. Some king had built it long ago on a little hill. You could still trace the stone causeways that led up to the ruined gates where the last splinters of wood hung to the worn, rusted hinges. Trees had grown into and out of the walls; the battlements were tumbled down and decayed, and wild creepers hung out of the windows of the towers on the walls in bushy hanging clumps.

A great roofless palace crowned the hill, and the marble of the courtyards and the fountains was split and stained with red and green, and the very cobblestones in the court-yard where the king's elephants used to live had been thrust up and apart by grasses and young trees. From the palace you could see the rows and rows of roofless houses that made up the city, looking like empty honey-combs filled with blackness; the shapeless block of stone that had been an idol in the square where four roads met; the pits and dimples at street corners where the public wells once stood, and the shattered domes of temples with wild figs sprouting on their sides.

The monkeys called the place their city, and pretended to despise the Jungle People because they lived in the forest. And yet they never knew what the buildings were made for nor how to use them. They would sit in circles on the hall of the king's council-chamber, and scratch for fleas and pretend to be men; or they would run in and out of the roofless houses and collect pieces of plaster and old bricks in a corner, and forget where they had hidden them, and fight and cry in scuffling crowds, and then break off to play up and down the terraces of the king's garden, where they would shake the rose-trees and the oranges in sport to see the fruit and flowers fall. They explored all the passages and dark tunnels in the palace and the hundreds of little dark rooms; but they never remembered what they had seen and what they had not, and so drifted about in ones and twos or crowds, telling one another that they were doing as men did. They drank at the tanks and made the water all muddy, and then they fought over it, and then they would all rush together in mobs and shout: "There are none in the jungle so wise and good and clever and strong and gentle as the Bandar-log." Then all would begin again till they grew tired of the city and went back to the tree-tops, hoping the Jungle People would notice them.

Mowgli, who had been trained under the Law of the Jungle, did not like or understand this kind of life. The monkeys dragged him into the Cold Lairs late in the afternoon, and instead of going to sleep, as Mowgli would have done after a long journey, they joined hands and danced about and sang their foolish songs.

One of the monkeys made a speech, and

told his companions that Mowgli's capture
marked a new thing in the history of the
Bandar-log, for Mowgli was going to show
them how to weave sticks and canes together
as a protection against rain and cold. Mowgli
picked up some creepers and began to work
them in and out, and the monkeys tried to imitate; but in a very few minutes they lost inter-
est and began to pull their friends' tails or
jump up and down on all fours, coughing.

"I want to eat," said Mowgli. "I am a
stranger in this part of the jungle. Bring me
food, or give me leave to hunt here."

Twenty or thirty monkeys bounded away to
bring him nuts and wild pawpaws; but they
fell to fighting on the road, and it was too
much trouble to go back with what was left of
the fruit. Mowgli was sore and angry as well
as hungry, and he roamed through the empty
city giving the Strangers' Hunting Call from
time to time, but no one answered him, and
Mowgli felt that he had reached a very bad
place indeed.

"All that Baloo has said about the Bandar-
log is true," he thought to himself. "They have
no Law, no Hunting Call, and no leaders—
nothing but foolish words and little picking,
thievish hands. So if I am starved or killed
here, it will be all my own fault. But I must try

to return to my own jungle. Baloo will surely beat me, but that is better than chasing silly rose-leaves with the Bandar-log."

But no sooner had he walked to the city wall than the monkeys pulled him back, telling him that he did not know how happy he was, and pinching him to make him grateful. He set his teeth and said nothing, but went with the shouting monkeys to a terrace above the red sandstone reservoirs that were half full of rain-water. There was a ruined summer-house of white marble in the center of the terrace, built for queens dead a hundred years ago. The domed roof had half fallen in and blocked up the underground passage from the palace by which the queens used to enter; but the walls were made of screens of marble tracery—beautiful, milk-white fretwork, set with agates and cornelians and jasper and lapis lazuli, and as the moon came up behind the hill it shone through the openwork, casting shadows on the ground like black-velvet embroidery.

Sore, sleepy, and hungry as he was, Mowgli could not help laughing when the Bandar-log began, twenty at a time, to tell him how great and wise and strong and gentle they were, and how foolish he was to wish to leave them. "We are great. We are free. We are wonderful.

We are the most wonderful people in all the jungle! We all say so, and so it must be true," they shouted. "Now as you are a new listener and can carry our words back to the Jungle People so that they may notice us in future, we will tell you all about our most excellent selves."

Mowgli made no objection, and the monkeys gathered by hundreds and hundreds on the terrace to listen to their own speakers singing the praises of the Bandar-log, and whenever a speaker stopped for want of breath they would all shout together: "This is true; we all say so."

Mowgli nodded and blinked, and said "Yes" when they asked him a question, and his head spun with the noise. "Tabaqui, the Jackal, must have bitten all these people," he said to himself, "and now they have the madness. Certainly this is *dewanee*—the madness. Do they never go to sleep? Now there is a cloud coming to cover that moon. If it were only a big enough cloud I might try to run away in the darkness. But I am tired."

That same cloud was being watched by two good friends in the ruined ditch below the city wall, for Bagheera and Kaa, knowing well how dangerous the Monkey People were in large numbers, did not wish to run any risks.

The monkeys never fight unless they are a hundred to one, and few in the jungle care for those odds.

"I will go to the west wall," Kaa whispered, "and come down swiftly with the slope of the ground in my favor. They will not throw themselves upon *my* back in their hundreds, but—"

"I know it," said Bagheera. "Would that Baloo were here; but we must do what we can. When that cloud covers the moon I shall go to the terrace. They hold some sort of council there over the boy."

"Good hunting," said Kaa, grimly, and glided away to the west wall. That happened to be the least ruined of any, and the big snake was delayed a while before he could find a way up the stones.

The cloud hid the moon, and as Mowgli wondered what would come next he heard Bagheera's light feet on the terrace. The Black Panther had raced up the slope almost without a sound, and was striking—he knew better than to waste time in biting—right and left among the monkeys, who were seated round Mowgli in circles fifty and sixty deep. There was a howl of fright and rage, and then as Bagheera tripped on the rolling, kicking bodies beneath him, a monkey shouted: "There is only one here! Kill him! Kill!" A scuffling mass

of monkeys, biting, scratching, tearing, and
pulling, closed over Bagheera, while five or
six laid hold of Mowgli, dragged him up the
wall of the summer-house, and pushed him
through the hole of the broken dome. A man-
trained boy would have been badly bruised,
for the fall was a good ten feet, but Mowgli
fell as Baloo had taught him to fall, and
landed light.

"Stay there," shouted the monkeys, "till we
have killed thy friend. Later we will play with
thee, if the Poison People leave thee alive."

"We be of one blood, ye and I," said Mowgli,
quickly giving the Snake's Call. He could hear
rustling and hissing in the rubbish all round
him, and gave the Call a second time to make
sure.

"Down hoods all," said half a dozen low
voices. Every old ruin in India becomes
sooner or later a dwelling-place of snakes,
and the old summer-house was alive with
cobras. "Stand still, Little Brother, lest thy
feet do us harm."

Mowgli stood as quietly as he could, peer-
ing through the openwork and listening to the
furious din of the fight round the Black
Panther—the yells and chatterings and scuf-
flings, and Bagheera's deep, hoarse cough as
he backed and bucked and twisted and

plunged under the heaps of his enemies. For the first time since he was born, Bagheera was fighting for his life.

"Baloo must be at hand; Bagheera would not have come alone," Mowgli thought; and then he called aloud: "To the tank, Bagheera! Roll to the water-tanks! Roll and plunge! Get to the water!"

Bagheera heard, and the cry that told him Mowgli was safe gave him new courage. He worked his way desperately, inch by inch, straight for the reservoirs, hitting in silence.

Then from the ruined wall nearest the jungle rose up the rumbling war-shout of Baloo. The old bear had done his best, but he could not come before. "Bagheera," he shouted, "I am here! I climb! I haste! *Ahuwora!* The stones slip under my feet! Wait my coming, O most infamous Bandar-log!"

He panted up the terrace only to disappear to the head in a wave of monkeys, but he threw himself squarely on his haunches, and spreading out his fore paws, hugged as many as he could hold, and then began to hit with a regular *bat-bat-bat*, like the flipping strokes of a paddlewheel.

A crash and a splash told Mowgli that Bagheera had fought his way to the tank, where the monkeys could not follow. The panther lay gasping for breath, his head just

out of water, while the monkeys stood three
deep on the red stone steps, dancing up and
down with rage, ready to spring upon him
from all sides if he came out to help Baloo. It
was then that Bagheera lifted up his dripping
chin, and in despair gave the Snake's Call for
protection,—"We be of one blood, ye and I,"—
for he believed that Kaa had turned tail at the
last minute. Even Baloo, half smothered
under the monkeys on the edge of the terrace,
could not help chuckling as he heard the big
Black Panther asking for help.

Kaa had only just worked his way over the
west wall, landing with a wrench that dis-
lodged a coping-stone into the ditch. He had
no intention of losing any advantage of the
ground, and coiled and uncoiled himself once
or twice, to be sure that every foot of his long
body was in working order.

All that while the fight with Baloo went on,
and the monkeys yelled in the tank round
Bagheera, and Mang, the Bat, flying to and fro,
carried the news of the great battle over the
jungle, till even Hathi, the Wild Elephant,
trumpeted, and, far away, scattered bands of
the Monkey Folk woke and came leaping
along the tree-roads to help their comrades in
the Cold Lairs, and the noise of the fight
roused all the day-birds for miles round.

Then Kaa came straight, quickly, and anxious to kill. The fighting strength of a python is in the driving blow of his head, backed by all the strength and weight of his body. If you can imagine a lance, or a battering-ram, or a hammer, weighing nearly half a ton driven by a cool, quiet mind living in the handle of it, you can imagine roughly what Kaa was like when he fought. A python four or five feet long can knock a man down if he hits him fairly in the chest, and Kaa was thirty feet long, as you know. His first stroke was delivered into the heart of the crowd round Baloo—was sent home with shut mouth in silence, and there was no need of a second. The monkeys scattered with cries of "Kaa! It is Kaa! Run! Run!"

Generations of monkeys had been scared into good behavior by the stories their elders told them of Kaa, the night-thief, who could slip along the branches as quietly as moss grows, and steal away the strongest monkey that ever lived; of old Kaa, who could make himself look so like a dead branch or a rotten stump that the wisest were deceived till the branch caught them, and then—

Kaa was everything that the monkeys feared in the jungle, for none of them knew the limits of his power, none of them could look him in the face, and none had ever come

"Kaa! It is Kaa! Run! Run!"

alive out of his hug. And so they ran, stammering with terror, to the walls and the roofs of the houses, and Baloo drew a deep breath of relief. His fur was much thicker than Bagheera's, but he had suffered sorely in the fight. Then Kaa opened his mouth for the first time and spoke one long hissing word, and the far-away monkeys, hurrying to the defense of the Cold Lairs, stayed where they were, cowering, till the loaded branches bent and crackled under them. The monkeys on the walls and the empty houses stopped their cries, and in the stillness that fell upon the city Mowgli heard Bagheera shaking his wet sides as he came up from the tank.

Then the clamor broke out again. The monkeys leaped higher up the walls; they clung round the necks of the big stone idols and shrieked as they skipped along the battlements; while Mowgli, dancing in the summerhouse, put his eye to the screenwork and hooted owl-fashion between his front teeth, to show his derision and contempt.

"Get the man-cub out of that trap; I can do no more," Bagheera gasped. "Let us take the man-cub and go. They may attack again."

"They will not move till I order them. Stay you sssso!" Kaa hissed, and the city was silent once more. "I could not come before, Brother, but I *think* I heard thee call"—this was to Bagheera.

"I—I may have cried out in the battle," Bagheera answered. "Baloo, art thou hurt?"

"I am not sure that they have not pulled me into a hundred little bearlings," said Baloo, gravely shaking one leg after the other. "Wow! I am sore. Kaa, we owe thee, I think, our lives—Bagheera and I."

"No matter. Where is the manling?"

"Here, in a trap. I cannot climb out," cried Mowgli. The curve of the broken dome was above his head.

"Take him away. He dances like Mao, the Peacock. He will crush our young," said the cobras inside.

"Hah!" said Kaa, with a chuckle, "he has friends everywhere, this manling. Stand back, Manling; and hide you, O Poison People. I break down the wall."

Kaa looked carefully till he found a discolored crack in the marble tracery showing a weak spot, made two or three light taps with his head to get the distance, and then lifting up six feet of his body clear of the ground, sent home half a dozen full-power, smashing blows, nose-first. The screenwork broke and fell away in a cloud of dust and rubbish, and Mowgli leaped through the opening and flung himself between Baloo and Bagheera—an arm round each big neck.

"Art thou hurt?" said Baloo, hugging him softly.

"I am sore, hungry, and not a little bruised; but, oh, they have handled ye grievously, my Brothers! Ye bleed."

"Others also," said Bagheera, licking his lips and looking at the monkey-dead on the terrace and round the tank.

"It is nothing, it is nothing if thou art safe, O my pride of all little frogs!" whimpered Baloo.

"Of that we shall judge later," said Bagheera, in a dry voice that Mowgli did not at all like. "But here is Kaa, to whom we owe the battle and thou owest thy life. Thank him according to our customs, Mowgli."

Mowgli turned and saw the great python's head swaying a foot above his own.

"So this is the manling," said Kaa. "Very soft is his skin, and he is not so unlike the Bandar-log. Have a care, Manling, that I do not mistake thee for a monkey some twilight when I have newly changed my coat."

"We be of one blood, thou and I," Mowgli answered. "I take my life from thee, to-night. My kill shall be thy kill if ever thou art hungry, O Kaa."

"All thanks, Little Brother," said Kaa,

though his eyes twinkled. "And what may so bold a hunter kill? I ask that I may follow when next he goes abroad."

"I kill nothing,—I am too little,—but I drive goats toward such as can use them. When thou art empty come to me and see if I speak the truth. I have some skill in these [he held out his hands], and if ever thou art in a trap, I may pay the debt which I owe to thee, to Bagheera, and to Baloo, here. Good hunting to ye all, my masters."

"Well said," growled Baloo, for Mowgli had returned thanks very prettily. The python dropped his head lightly for a minute on Mowgli's shoulder. "A brave heart and a courteous tongue," said he. "They shall carry thee far through the jungle, Manling. But now go hence quickly with thy friends. Go and sleep, for the moon sets, and what follows it is not well that thou shouldst see."

The moon was sinking behind the hills and the lines of trembling monkeys huddled together on the walls and battlements looked like ragged, shaky fringes of things. Baloo went down to the tank for a drink, and Bagheera began to put his fur in order, as Kaa glided out into the center of the terrace and brought his jaws together with a ringing snap that drew all the monkeys' eyes upon him.

"The moon sets," he said. "Is there yet light to see?"

From the walls came a moan like the wind in the tree-tops: "We see, O Kaa!"

"Good! Begins now the Dance—the Dance of the Hunger of Kaa. Sit still and watch."

He turned twice or thrice in a big circle, weaving his head from right to left. Then he began making loops and figures of eight with his body, and soft, oozy triangles that melted into squares and five-sided figures, and coiled mounds, never resting, never hurrying, and never stopping his low, humming song. It grew darker and darker, till at last the dragging, shifting coils disappeared, but they could hear the rustle of the scales.

Baloo and Bagheera stood still as stone, growling in their throats, their neck-hair bristling, and Mowgli watched and wondered.

"Bandar-log," said the voice of Kaa at last, "can ye stir foot or hand without my order? Speak!"

"Without thy order we cannot stir foot or hand, O Kaa!"

"Good! Come all one pace nearer to me."

The lines of the monkeys swayed forward helplessly, and Baloo and Bagheera took one stiff step forward with them.

"Nearer!" hissed Kaa, and they all moved again.

Mowgli laid his hands on Baloo and Bagheera to get them away, and the two great beasts started as though they had been waked from a dream.

"Keep thy hand on my shoulder," Bagheera whispered. "Keep it there, or I must go back—must go back to Kaa. *Aah!*"

"It is only old Kaa making circles on the dust," said Mowgli; "let us go"; and the three slipped off through a gap in the walls to the jungle.

"*Whoof!*" said Baloo, when he stood under the still trees again. "Never more will I make an ally of Kaa," and he shook himself all over.

"He knows more than we," said Bagheera, trembling. "In a little time, had I stayed, I should have walked down his throat."

"Many will walk that road before the moon rises again," said Baloo. "He will have good hunting—after his own fashion."

"But what was the meaning of it all?" said Mowgli, who did not know anything of a python's powers of fascination. "I saw no more than a big snake making foolish circles till the dark came. And his nose was all sore. Ho! Ho!"

"Mowgli," said Bagheera, angrily, "his nose was sore on *thy* account; as my ears and sides and paws, and Baloo's neck and shoulders are bitten on *thy* account. Neither Baloo nor Bagheera will be able to hunt with pleasure for many days."

"It is nothing," said Baloo; "we have the man-cub again."

"True; but he has cost us most heavily in time which might have been spent in good hunting, in wounds, in hair,—I am half plucked along my back,—and last of all, in honor. For, remember, Mowgli, I, who am the Black Panther, was forced to call upon Kaa for protection, and Baloo and I were both made stupid as little birds by the Hunger-Dance. All this, Man-cub, came of thy playing with the Bandar-log."

"True; it is true," said Mowgli, sorrowfully. "I am an evil man-cub, and my stomach is sad in me."

"*Mf!* What says the Law of the Jungle, Baloo?"

Baloo did not wish to bring Mowgli into any more trouble, but he could not tamper with the Law, so he mumbled, "Sorrow never stays punishment. But remember, Bagheera, he is very little."

"I will remember; but he has done mischief; and blows must be dealt now. Mowgli, hast thou anything to say?"

"Nothing. I did wrong. Baloo and thou art wounded. It is just."

Bagheera gave him half a dozen love-taps; from a panther's point of view they would hardly have waked one of his own cubs, but for a seven year-old boy they amounted to as severe a beating as you could wish to avoid. When it was all over Mowgli sneezed, and picked himself up without a word.

"Now," said Bagheera, "jump on my back, Little Brother, and we will go home."

One of the beauties of Jungle Law is that punishment settles all scores. There is no nagging afterward.

Mowgli laid his head down on Bagheera's back and slept so deeply that he never waked when he was put down by Mother Wolf's side in the home-cave.

ROAD-SONG OF THE BANDAR-LOG

Here we go in a flung festoon,
Half-way up to the jealous moon!
Don't you envy our pranceful bands?
Don't you wish you had extra hands?
Would n't you like if your tails were —*so*—

Curved in the shape of a Cupid's bow?
> Now you 're angry, but—never mind,
> *Brother, thy tail hangs down behind!*

Here we sit in a branchy row,
Thinking of beautiful things we know;
Dreaming of deeds that we mean to do,
All complete, in a minute or two—
Something noble and grand and good,
Won by merely wishing we could.
> Now we're going to—never mind,
> *Brother, thy tail hangs down behind!*

All the talk we ever have heard
Uttered by bat or beast or bird—
Hide or fin or scale or feather—
Jabber it quickly and all together!
Excellent! Wonderful! Once again!
Now we are talking just like men.
> Let's pretend we are . . . never mind,
> *Brother, thy tail hangs down behind!*
> This is the way of the Monkey-kind.

*Then join our leaping lines that scumfish
through the pines,*
*That rocket by where, light and high, the wild-
grape swings.*
*By the rubbish in our wake, and the noble noise
we make,*
*Be sure, be sure, we're going to do some splendid
things!*

"Tiger! Tiger!"

What of the hunting, hunter bold?
Brother, the watch was long and cold.
What of the quarry ye went to kill?
Brother, he crops in the jungle still.
Where is the power that made your pride:
Brother, it ebbs from my flank and side.
Where is the haste that ye hurry by?
Brother, I go to my lair—to die.

"Tiger! Tiger!"

NOW WE MUST GO back to the last tale but one. When Mowgli left the wolf's cave after the fight with the Pack at the Council Rock, he went down to the plowed lands where the villagers lived, but he would not stop there because it was too near to the jungle, and he knew that he had made at least one bad enemy at the Council. So he hurried on, keeping to the rough road that ran down the valley, and followed it at a steady jog-trot for nearly twenty miles, till he came to a country that he did not know. The valley opened out into a great plain dotted over with rocks and cut up by ravines. At one end stood a little village, and at the other the thick jungle came down in a sweep to the grazing-grounds, and stopped there as though it had been cut off with a hoe. All over the plain, cattle and buffaloes were grazing, and when the little boys in charge of the herds saw Mowgli they shouted and ran away, and the yellow pariah dogs that hang about every Indian village barked. Mowgli walked on, for he was feeling hungry, and when he came to the village gate he saw the big thorn-bush that was drawn up before the gate at twilight, pushed to one side.

"Umph!" he said, for he had come across more than one such barricade in his night rambles after things to eat. "So men are afraid of the People of the Jungle here also." He sat down by the gate, and when a man came out he stood up, opened his mouth, and pointed down it to show that he wanted food. The man stared, and ran back up the one street of the village shouting for the priest, who was a big, fat man dressed in white, with a red and yellow mark on his forehead. The priest came to the gate, and with him at least a hundred people, who stared and talked and shouted and pointed at Mowgli.

"They have no manners, these Men Folk," said Mowgli to himself. "Only the gray ape would behave as they do." So he threw back his long hair and frowned at the crowd.

"What is there to be afraid of?" said the priest. "Look at the marks on his arms and legs. They are the bites of wolves. He is but a wolf-child run away from the jungle."

Of course, in playing together, the cubs had

often nipped Mowgli harder than they intended, and there were white scars all over his arms and legs. But he would have been the last person in the world to call these bites; for he knew what real biting meant.

"*Arré! Arré!*" said two or three women together. "To be bitten by wolves, poor child! He is a handsome boy. He has eyes like red fire. By my honor, Messua, he is not unlike thy boy that was taken by the tiger."

"Let me look," said a woman with heavy copper rings on her wrists and ankles, and she peered at Mowgli under the palm of her hand. "Indeed he is not. He is thinner, but he has the very look of my boy."

The priest was a clever man, and he knew that Messua was wife to the richest villager in the place. So he looked up at the sky for a minute, and said solemnly: "What the jungle has taken the jungle has restored. Take the boy into thy house, my sister, and forget not to honor the priest who sees so far into the lives of men."

"By the Bull that bought me," said Mowgli to himself, "but all this talking is like another looking-over by the Pack! Well, if I am a man, a man I must become."

The crowd parted as the woman beckoned Mowgli to her hut, where there was a red lacquered bedstead, a great earthen grain-chest with curious raised patterns on it, half a dozen copper cooking-pots, an image of a Hindu god in a little alcove, and on the wall a real looking-glass, such as they sell at the country fairs.

She gave him a long drink of milk and some bread, and then she laid her hand on his head and looked into his eyes; for she thought perhaps that he might be her real son come back from the jungle where the tiger had taken him. So she said: "Nathoo, O Nathoo!" Mowgli did not show that he knew the name. "Dost thou not remember the day when I gave thee thy new shoes?" She touched his foot, and it was almost as hard as horn. "No," she said, sorrowfully; "those feet have never worn shoes, but thou art very like my Nathoo, and thou shalt be my son."

Mowgli was uneasy, because he had never been under a roof before; but as he looked at the thatch, he saw that he could tear it out any time if he wanted to get away, and that the window had no fastenings. "What is the good of a man," he said to himself at last, "if he does not understand man's talk? Now I am as silly and dumb as a man would be with us in the jungle. I must learn their talk."

It was not for fun that he had learned while

he was with the wolves to imitate the challenge of bucks in the jungle and the grunt of the little wild pig. So as soon as Messua pronounced a word Mowgli would imitate it almost perfectly, and before dark he had learned the names of many things in the hut.

There was a difficulty at bedtime, because Mowgli would not sleep under anything that looked so like a panther-trap as that hut, and when they shut the door he went through the window. "Give him his will," said Messua's husband. "Remember he can never till now have slept on a bed. If he is indeed sent in the place of our son he will not run away."

So Mowgli stretched himself in some long, clean grass at the edge of the field, but before he had closed his eyes a soft gray nose poked him under the chin.

"Phew!" said Gray Brother (he was the eldest of Mother Wolf's cubs). "This is a poor reward for following thee twenty miles. Thou smellest of wood-smoke and cattle—altogether like a man already. Wake, Little Brother; I bring news."

"Are all well in the jungle?" said Mowgli, hugging him.

"All except the wolves that were burned with the Red Flower. Now, listen. Shere Khan has gone away to hunt far off till his coat

grows again, for he is badly singed. When he
returns he swears that he will lay thy bones in
the Waingunga."

"There are two words to that. I also have
made a little promise. But news is always
good. I am tired to-night,—very tired with
new things, Gray Brother,—but bring me the
news always."

"Thou wilt not forget that thou art a wolf?
Men will not make thee forget?" said Gray
Brother, anxiously.

"Never. I will always remember that I love
thee and all in our cave; but also I will always
remember that I have been cast out of the
Pack."

"And that thou mayest be cast out of
another pack. Men are only men, Little
Brother, and their talk is like the talk of frogs
in a pond. When I come down here again, I
will wait for thee in the bamboos at the edge
of the grazing-ground."

For three months after that night Mowgli
hardly ever left the village gate, he was so
busy learning the ways and customs of men.
First he had to wear a cloth round him, which
annoyed him horribly; and then he had to
learn about money, which he did not in the
least understand, and about plowing, of which
he did not see the use. Then the little children

in the village made him very angry. Luckily, the Law of the Jungle had taught him to keep his temper, for in the jungle, life and food depend on keeping your temper; but when they made fun of him because he would not play games or fly kites, or because he mispronounced some word, only the knowledge that it was unsportsmanlike to kill little naked cubs kept him from picking them up and breaking them in two.

He did not know his own strength in the least. In the jungle he knew he was weak compared with the beasts, but in the village, people said he was as strong as a bull.

And Mowgli had not the faintest idea of the difference that caste makes between man and man. When the potter's donkey slipped in the clay-pit, Mowgli hauled it out by the tail, and helped to stack the pots for their journey to the market at Khanhiwara. That was very shocking, too, for the potter is a low-caste man, and his donkey is worse. When the priest scolded him, Mowgli threatened to put him on the donkey, too, and the priest told Messua's husband that Mowgli had better be set to work as soon as possible; and the village head-man told Mowgli that he would have to go out with the buffaloes next day, and herd them while they grazed. No one was more pleased than Mowgli; and that night, because he had been appointed a servant of the village, as it were, he went off to a circle that met every evening on a masonry platform under a great fig-tree. It was the village club, and the head-man and the watchman and the barber (who knew all the gossip of the village), and old Buldeo, the village hunter, who had a Tower musket, met and smoked. The monkeys sat and talked in the upper branches, and there was a hole under the platform where a cobra lived, and he had his little platter of milk every night because he was sacred; and the old men sat around the tree and talked, and pulled at the big *huqas* (the water-pipes) till far into the night. They told wonderful tales of gods and men and ghosts; and Buldeo told even more wonderful ones of the ways of beasts in the jungle, till the eyes of the children sitting outside the circle bulged out of their heads. Most of the tales were about animals, for the jungle was always at their door. The deer and the wild pig grubbed up their crops, and now and again the tiger carried off a man at twilight, within sight of the village gates.

Mowgli, who naturally knew something about what they were talking of, had to cover his face not to show that he was laughing,

Mowgli had to cover his face not to show that he
was laughing.

while Buldeo, the Tower musket across his
knees, climbed on from one wonderful story
to another, and Mowgli's shoulders shook.

Buldeo was explaining how the tiger that
had carried away Messua's son was a ghost-
tiger, and his body was inhabited by the ghost
of a wicked old money-lender, who had died
some years ago. "And I know that this is true,"
he said, "because Purun Dass always limped
from the blow that he got in a riot when his
account-books were burned, and the tiger that
I speak of *he* limps, too, for the tracks of his
pads are unequal."

"True, true; that must be the truth," said the
graybeards, nodding together.

"Are all these tales such cobwebs and
moon-talk?" said Mowgli. "That tiger limps
because he was born lame, as every one
knows. To talk of the soul of a money-lender
in a beast that never had the courage of a
jackal is child's talk."

Buldeo was speechless with surprise for a
moment, and the head-man stared.

"Oho! It is the jungle brat, is it?" said
Buldeo. "If thou art so wise, better bring his
hide to Khanhiwara, for the Government has
set a hundred rupees [$30] on his life. Better
still, do not talk when thy elders speak."

Mowgli rose to go. "All the evening I have

lain here listening," he called back over his
shoulder, "and, except once or twice, Buldeo
has not said one word of truth concerning the
jungle, which is at his very doors. How, then,
shall I believe the tales of ghosts and gods
and goblins which he says he has seen?"

"It is full time that boy went to herding,"
said the head-man, while Buldeo puffed and
snorted at Mowgli's impertinence.

The custom of most Indian villages is for a
few boys to take the cattle and buffaloes out
to graze in the early morning, and bring them
back at night; and the very cattle that would
trample a white man to death allow themselves to be banged and bullied and shouted
at by children that hardly come up to their
noses. So long as the boys keep with the
herds they are safe, for not even the tiger will
charge a mob of cattle. But if they straggle to
pick flowers or hunt lizards, they are sometimes carried off. Mowgli went through the
village street in the dawn, sitting on the back
of Rama, the great herd bull; and the slaty-
blue buffaloes, with their long, backward-
sweeping horns and savage eyes, rose out of
their byres, one by one, and followed him, and
Mowgli made it very clear to the children with
him that he was the master. He beat the buffaloes with a long, polished bamboo, and told

Kamya, one of the boys, to graze the cattle by themselves, while he went on with the buffaloes, and to be very careful not to stray away from the herd.

An Indian grazing-ground is all rocks and scrub and tussocks and little ravines, among which the herds scatter and disappear. The buffaloes generally keep to the pools and muddy places, where they lie wallowing or basking in the warm mud for hours. Mowgli drove them on to the edge of the plain where the Waingunga River came out of the jungle; then he dropped from Rama's neck, trotted off to a bamboo clump, and found Gray Brother. "Ah," said Gray Brother, "I have waited here very many days. What is the meaning of this cattle-herding work?"

"It is an order," said Mowgli. "I am a village herd for a while. What news of Shere Khan?"

"He has come back to this country, and has waited here a long time for thee. Now he has gone off again, for the game is scarce. But he means to kill thee."

"Very good," said Mowgli. "So long as he is away do thou or one of the brothers sit on that rock, so that I can see thee as I come out of the village. When he comes back wait for me in the ravine by the *dhâk*-tree in the center of the plain. We need not walk into Shere Khan's mouth."

Then Mowgli picked out a shady place, and lay down and slept while the buffaloes grazed round him. Herding in India is one of the laziest things in the world. The cattle move and crunch, and lie down, and move on again, and they do not even low. They only grunt, and the buffaloes very seldom say anything, but get down into the muddy pools one after another, and work their way into the mud till only their noses and staring china-blue eyes show above the surface, and there they lie like logs. The sun makes the rocks dance in the heat, and the herd-children hear one kite (never any more) whistling almost out of sight overhead, and they know that if they died, or a cow died, that kite would sweep down, and the next kite miles away would see him drop and follow, and the next, and the next, and almost before they were dead there would be a score of hungry kites come out of nowhere. Then they sleep and wake and sleep again, and weave little baskets of dried grass and put grasshoppers in them; or catch two praying-mantises and make them fight; or string a necklace of red and black jungle-nuts; or watch a lizard basking on a rock, or a

snake hunting a frog near the wallows. Then
they sing long, long songs with odd native
quavers at the end of them, and the day seems
longer than most people's whole lives, and
perhaps they make a mud castle with mud figures of men and horses and buffaloes, and put
reeds into the men's hands, and pretend that
they are kings and the figures are their
armies, or that they are gods to be worshiped.
Then evening comes, and the children call,
and the buffaloes lumber up out of the sticky
mud with noises like gunshots going off one
after the other, and they all string across the
gray plain back to the twinkling village lights.

Day after day Mowgli would lead the buffaloes out to their wallows, and day after day he
would see Gray Brother's back a mile and a
half away across the plain (so he knew that
Shere Khan had not come back), and day after
day he would lie on the grass listening to the
noise round him, and dreaming of old days in
the jungle. If Shere Khan had made a false
step with his lame paw up in the jungles by
the Waingunga, Mowgli would have heard him
in those long still mornings.

At last a day came when he did not see
Gray Brother at the signal place, and he
laughed and headed the buffaloes for the

ravine by the *dhâk*-tree, which was all covered with golden-red flowers. There sat Gray Brother, every bristle on his back lifted.

"He has hidden for a month to throw thee off thy guard. He crossed the ranges last night with Tabaqui, hot-foot on thy trail," said the wolf, panting.

Mowgli frowned. "I am not afraid of Shere Khan, but Tabaqui is very cunning."

"Have no fear," said Gray Brother, licking his lips a little. "I met Tabaqui in the dawn. Now he is telling all his wisdom to the kites, but he told *me* everything before I broke his back. Shere Khan's plan is to wait for thee at the village gate this evening—for thee and for no one else. He is lying up now in the big dry ravine of the Waingunga."

"Has he eaten to-day, or does he hunt empty?" said Mowgli, for the answer meant life or death to him.

"He killed at dawn,—a pig,—and he has drunk too. Remember, Shere Khan could never fast even for the sake of revenge."

"Oh! Fool, fool! What a cub's cub it is! Eaten and drunk too, and he thinks that I shall wait till he has slept! Now, where does he lie up? If there were but ten of us we might pull him down as he lies. These buffaloes will not charge unless they wind him, and I cannot speak their language. Can we get behind his track so that they may smell it?"

"He swam far down the Waingunga to cut that off," said Gray Brother.

"Tabaqui told him that, I know. He would never have thought of it alone." Mowgli stood with his finger in his mouth, thinking. "The big ravine of the Waingunga. That opens out on the plain not half a mile from here. I can take the herd round through the jungle to the head of the ravine and then sweep down—but he would slink out at the foot. We must block that end. Gray Brother, canst thou cut the herd in two for me?"

"Not I, perhaps—but I have brought a wise helper." Gray Brother trotted off and dropped into a hole. Then there lifted up a huge gray head that Mowgli knew well, and the hot air was filled with the most desolate cry of all the jungle—the hunting-howl of a wolf at midday.

"Akela! Akela!" said Mowgli, clapping his hands. "I might have known that thou wouldst not forget me. We have a big work in hand. Cut the herd in two, Akela. Keep the cows and calves together, and the bulls and the plow-buffaloes by themselves."

The two wolves ran, ladies'-chain fashion, in and out of the herd, which snorted and threw up its head, and separated into two clumps. In one the cow-buffaloes stood, with their calves in the center, and glared and pawed, ready, if a wolf would only stay still, to charge down and trample the life out of him. In the other the bulls and the young bulls snorted and stamped; but, though they looked more imposing, they were much less dangerous, for they had no calves to protect. No six men could have divided the herd so neatly.

"What orders!" panted Akela. "They are trying to join again."

Mowgli slipped on to Rama's back. "Drive the bulls away to the left, Akela. Gray Brother, when we are gone hold the cows together, and drive them into the foot of the ravine."

"How far?" said Gray Brother, panting and snapping.

"Till the sides are higher than Shere Khan can jump," shouted Mowgli. "Keep them there till we come down." The bulls swept off as Akela bayed, and Gray Brother stopped in front of the cows. They charged down on him, and he ran just before them to the foot of the ravine, as Akela drove the bulls far to the left.

"Well done! Another charge and they are fairly started. Careful, now—careful, Akela. A snap too much, and the bulls will charge. *Hujah!* This is wilder work than driving black-buck. Didst thou think these creatures could move so swiftly?" Mowgli called.

"I have—have hunted these too in my time," gasped Akela in the dust. "Shall I turn them into the jungle?"

"Ay, turn! Swiftly turn them. Rama is mad with rage. Oh, if I could only tell him what I need of him to-day!"

The bulls were turned to the right this time, and crashed into the standing thicket. The other herd-children, watching with the cattle half a mile away, hurried to the village as fast as their legs could carry them, crying that the buffaloes had gone mad and run away.

But Mowgli's plan was simple enough. All he wanted to do was to make a big circle uphill and get at the head of the ravine, and then take the bulls down it and catch Shere Khan between the bulls and the cows, for he knew that after a meal and a full drink Shere Khan would not be in any condition to fight or to clamber up the sides of the ravine. He was soothing the buffaloes now by voice, and Akela had dropped far to the rear, only whimpering once or twice to hurry the rear-guard. It was a long, long circle, for they did not wish to get too near the ravine and give Shere Khan warning. At last Mowgli rounded up the bewildered herd at the head of the ravine on a grassy patch that sloped steeply down to the ravine itself. From that height you could see across the tops of the trees down to the plain below; but what Mowgli looked at was the sides of the ravine, and he saw with a great deal of satisfaction that they ran nearly straight up and down, and the vines and creepers that hung over them would give no foothold to a tiger who wanted to get out.

"Let them breathe, Akela," he said, holding up his hand. "They have not winded him yet. Let them breathe. I must tell Shere Khan who comes. We have him in the trap."

He put his hands to his mouth and shouted down the ravine,—it was almost like shouting down a tunnel,—and the echoes jumped from rock to rock.

After a long time there came back the drawling, sleepy snarl of a full-fed tiger just awakened.

"Who calls?" said Shere Khan, and a splendid peacock fluttered up out of the ravine, screeching.

"I, Mowgli. Cattle-thief, it is time to come to the Council Rock! Down—hurry them down, Akela. Down, Rama, down!"

The herd paused for an instant at the edge of the slope, but Akela gave tongue in the full hunting-yell, and they pitched over one after the other just as steamers shoot rapids, the sand and stones spurting up round them. Once started, there was no chance of stopping, and before they were fairly in the bed of the ravine Rama winded Shere Khan and bellowed.

"Ha! Ha!" said Mowgli, on his back. "Now thou knowest!" and the torrent of black horns, foaming muzzles, and staring eyes whirled down the ravine like boulders in flood-time; the weaker buffaloes being shouldered out to the sides of the ravine where they tore through the creepers. They knew what the business was before them—the terrible charge of the buffalo-herd, against which no tiger can hope to stand. Shere Khan heard the thunder of their hoofs, picked himself up, and lumbered down the ravine, looking from side to side for some way of escape, but the walls of the ravine were straight, and he had to keep on, heavy with his dinner and his drink, willing to do anything rather than fight. The herd splashed through the pool he had just left, bellowing till the narrow cut rang. Mowgli heard an answering bellow from the foot of the ravine, saw Shere Khan turn (the tiger knew if the worst came to the worst it was better to meet the bulls than the cows with their calves), and then Rama tripped, stumbled, and went on again over something soft, and, with the bulls at his heels, crashed full into the other herd, while the weaker buffaloes were lifted clean off their feet by the shock of the meeting. That charge carried both herds out into the plain, goring and stamping and snorting. Mowgli watched his time, and slipped off Rama's neck, laying about him right and left with his stick.

"Quick, Akela! Break them up. Scatter them, or they will be fighting one another. Drive them away, Akela. *Hai*, Rama! *Hai! hai! hai!* my children. Softly now, softly! It is all over."

Akela and Gray Brother ran to and fro nipping the buffaloes' legs, and though the herd wheeled once to charge up the ravine again, Mowgli managed to turn Rama, and the others followed him to the wallows.

Shere Khan needed no more trampling. He was dead, and the kites were coming for him already.

"Brothers, that was a dog's death," said Mowgli, feeling for the knife he always carried in a sheath round his neck now that he lived with men. "But he would never have shown fight. His hide will look well on the Council Rock. We must get to work swiftly."

A boy trained among men would never have

dreamed of skinning a ten-foot tiger alone, but Mowgli knew better than any one else how an animal's skin is fitted on, and how it can be taken off. But it was hard work, and Mowgli slashed and tore and grunted for an hour, while the wolves lolled out their tongues, or came forward and tugged as he ordered them.

Presently a hand fell on his shoulder, and looking up he saw Buldeo with the Tower musket. The children had told the village about the buffalo stampede, and Buldeo went out angrily, only too anxious to correct Mowgli for not taking better care of the herd. The wolves dropped out of sight as soon as they saw the man coming.

"What is this folly?" said Buldeo, angrily. "To think that thou canst skin a tiger! Where did the buffaloes kill him? It is the Lame Tiger, too, and there is a hundred rupees on his head. Well, well, we will overlook thy letting the herd run off, and perhaps I will give thee one of the rupees of the reward when I have taken the skin to Khanhiwara." He fumbled in his waist-cloth for flint and steel, and stooped down to singe Shere Khan's whiskers. Most native hunters singe a tiger's whiskers to prevent his ghost haunting them.

"Hum!" said Mowgli, half to himself as he

ripped back the skin of a fore paw. "So thou wilt take the hide to Khanhiwara for the reward, and perhaps give me one rupee? Now it is in my mind that I need the skin for my own use. Heh! old man, take away that fire!"

"What talk is this to the chief hunter of the village? Thy luck and the stupidity of thy buffaloes have helped thee to this kill. The tiger has just fed, or he would have gone twenty miles by this time. Thou canst not even skin him properly, little beggar-brat, and forsooth I, Buldeo, must be told not to singe his whiskers. Mowgli, I will not give thee one anna of the reward, but only a very big beating. Leave the carcass!"

"By the Bull that bought me," said Mowgli, who was trying to get at the shoulder, "must I stay babbling to an old ape all noon? Here, Akela, this man plagues me."

Buldeo, who was still stooping over Shere Khan's head, found himself sprawling on the grass, with a gray wolf standing over him, while Mowgli went on skinning as though he were alone in all India.

"Ye-es," he said, between his teeth. "Thou art altogether right, Buldeo. Thou wilt never give me one anna of the reward. There is an old war between this lame tiger and myself— a very old war, and—I have won."

To do Buldeo justice, if he had been ten years younger he would have taken his chance with Akela had he met the wolf in the woods, but a wolf who obeyed the orders of this boy who had private wars with man-eating tigers was not a common animal. It was sorcery, magic of the worst kind, thought Buldeo, and he wondered whether the amulet round his neck would protect him. He lay as still as still, expecting every minute to see Mowgli turn into a tiger, too.

"Maharaj! Great King," he said at last, in a husky whisper.

"Yes," said Mowgli, without turning his head, chuckling a little.

"I am an old man. I did not know that thou wast anything more than a herd-boy. May I rise up and go away, or will thy servant tear me to pieces?"

"Go, and peace go with thee. Only, another time do not meddle with my game. Let him go, Akela."

Buldeo hobbled away to the village as fast as he could, looking back over his shoulder in case Mowgli should change into something terrible. When he got to the village he told a tale of magic and enchantment and sorcery that made the priest look very grave.

Mowgli went on with his work, but it was nearly twilight before he and the wolves had drawn the great gay skin clear of the body.

"Now we must hide this and take the buffaloes home! Help me to herd them, Akela."

The herd rounded up in the misty twilight, and when they got near the village Mowgli saw lights, and heard the conches and bells in the temple blowing and banging. Half the village seemed to be waiting for him by the gate. "That is because I have killed Shere Khan," he said to himself; but a shower of stones whistled about his ears, and the villagers shouted: "Sorcerer! Wolf's brat! Jungle-demon! Go away! Get hence quickly, or the priest will turn thee into a wolf again. Shoot, Buldeo, shoot!"

The old Tower musket went off with a bang, and a young buffalo bellowed in pain.

"More sorcery!" shouted the villagers. "He can turn bullets. Buldeo, that was *thy* buffalo."

"Now what is this?" said Mowgli, bewildered, as the stones flew thicker.

"They are not unlike the Pack, these brothers of thine," said Akela, sitting down composedly. "It is in my head that, if bullets mean anything, they would cast thee out."

"Wolf! Wolf's cub! Go away!" shouted the priest, waving a sprig of the sacred *tulsi* plant.

"Again? Last time it was because I was a man. This time it is because I am a wolf. Let us go, Akela."

A woman—it was Messua—ran across to the herd, and cried: "Oh, my son, my son! They say thou art a sorcerer who can turn himself into a beast at will. I do not believe, but go away or they will kill thee. Buldeo says thou art a wizard, but I know thou hast avenged Nathoo's death."

"Come back, Messua!" shouted the crowd. "Come back, or we will stone thee."

Mowgli laughed a little short ugly laugh, for a stone had hit him in the mouth. "Run back, Messua. This is one of the foolish tales they tell under the big tree at dusk. I have at least paid for thy son's life. Farewell; and run quickly, for I shall send the herd in more swiftly than their brickbats. I am no wizard, Messua. Farewell!

"Now, once more, Akela," he cried. "Bring the herd in."

The buffaloes were anxious enough to get to the village. They hardly needed Akela's yell, but charged through the gate like a whirlwind, scattering the crowd right and left.

"Keep count!" shouted Mowgli, scornfully. "It may be that I have stolen one of them. Keep count, for I will do your herding no more. Fare you well, children of men, and thank Messua that I do not come in with my wolves and hunt you up and down your street."

He turned on his heel and walked away with the Lone Wolf; and as he looked up at the stars he felt happy. "No more sleeping in traps for me, Akela. Let us get Shere Khan's skin and go away. No; we will not hurt the village, for Messua was kind to me."

When the moon rose over the plain, making it look all milky, the horrified villagers saw Mowgli, with two wolves at his heels and a bundle on his head, trotting across at the steady wolf's trot that eats up the long miles like fire. Then they banged the temple bells and blew the conches louder than ever; and Messua cried, and Buldeo embroidered the story of his adventures in the jungle, till he ended by saying that Akela stood up on his hind legs and talked like a man.

The moon was just going down when Mowgli and the two wolves came to the hill of the Council Rock, and they stopped at Mother Wolf's cave.

"They have cast me out from the Man Pack,

Mother," shouted Mowgli, "but I come with the hide of Shere Khan to keep my word." Mother Wolf walked stiffly from the cave with the cubs behind her, and her eyes glowed as she saw the skin.

"I told him on that day, when he crammed his head and shoulders into this cave, hunting for thy life, Little Frog—I told him that the hunter would be the hunted. It is well done."

"Little Brother, it is well done," said a deep voice in the thicket. "We were lonely in the jungle without thee," and Bagheera came running to Mowgli's bare feet. They clambered up the Council Rock together, and Mowgli spread the skin out on the flat stone where Akela used to sit, and pegged it down with four slivers of bamboo, and Akela lay down upon it, and called the old call to the Council, "Look— look well, O Wolves!" exactly as he had called when Mowgli was first brought there.

Ever since Akela had been deposed, the Pack had been without a leader, hunting and fighting at their own pleasure. But they answered the call from habit, and some of them were lame from the traps they had fallen into, and some limped from shot-wounds, and some were mangy from eating bad food, and many were missing; but they came to the Council Rock, all that were left of them, and

Mowgli spread the skin out on the flat stone
where Akela used to sit.

saw Shere Khan's striped hide on the rock, and the huge claws dangling at the end of the empty, dangling feet. It was then that Mowgli made up a song without any rhymes, a song that came up into his throat all by itself, and he shouted it aloud, leaping up and down on the rattling skin, and beating time with his heels till he had no more breath left, while Gray Brother and Akela howled between the verses.

"Look well, O Wolves. Have I kept my word?" said Mowgli when he had finished; and the wolves bayed "Yes," and one tattered wolf howled:

"Lead us again, O Akela. Lead us again, O Man-cub, for we be sick of this lawlessness, and we would be the Free People once more."

"Nay," purred Bagheera, "that may not be. When ye are full-fed, the madness may come upon ye again. Not for nothing are ye called the Free People. Ye fought for freedom, and it is yours. Eat it, O Wolves."

"Man Pack and Wolf Pack have cast me out," said Mowgli. "Now I will hunt alone in the jungle."

"And we will hunt with thee," said the four cubs.

So Mowgli went away and hunted with the four cubs in the jungle from that day on. But

he was not always alone, because years afterward he became a man and married.

But that is a story for grown-ups.

MOWGLI'S SONG

THAT HE SANG AT THE COUNCIL ROCK WHEN HE
DANCED ON SHERE KHAN'S HIDE

The Song of Mowgli—I, Mowgli, am singing. Let
the jungle listen to the things I have done.

Shere Khan said he would kill—would kill! At the
gates in the twilight he would kill Mowgli, the
Frog!

He ate and he drank. Drink deep, Shere Khan, for
when wilt thou drink again? Sleep and dream
of the kill.

I am alone on the grazing-grounds. Gray Brother,
come to me! Come to me, Lone Wolf, for there
is big game afoot.

Bring up the great bull-buffaloes, the blue-skinned
herd-bulls with the angry eyes. Drive them to
and fro as I order.

Sleepest thou still, Shere Khan? Wake, O wake!
Here come I, and the bulls are behind.

Rama, the King of the Buffaloes, stamped with his
foot. Waters of the Waingunga, whither went
Shere Khan?

He is not Ikki to dig holes, nor Mao, the Peacock,
that he should fly. He is not Mang, the Bat, to
hang in the branches. Little bamboos that
creak together, tell me where he ran?

Ow! He is there. *Ahoo!* He is there. Under the feet

of Rama lies the Lame One! Up, Shere Khan!
Up and kill! Here is meat; break the necks of
the bulls!

Hsh! He is asleep. We will not wake him, for his
strength is very great. The kites have come
down to see it. The black ants have come up
to know it. There is a great assembly in his
honor.

Alala! I have no cloth to wrap me. The kites will
see that I am naked. I am ashamed to meet all
these people.

Lend me thy coat, Shere Khan. Lend me thy gay
striped coat that I may go to the Council
Rock.

By the Bull that bought me I have made a
promise—a little promise. Only thy coat is
lacking before I keep my word.

With the knife—with the knife that men use—with
the knife of the hunter, the man, I will stoop
down for my gift.

Waters of the Waingunga, bear witness that Shere
Khan gives me his coat for the love that he
bears me. Pull, Gray Brother! Pull, Akela!
Heavy is the hide of Shere Khan.

The Man Pack are angry. They throw stones and
talk child's talk. My mouth is bleeding. Let us
run away.

Through the night, through the hot night, run
swiftly with me, my brothers. We will leave
the lights of the village and go to the low
moon.

Waters of the Waingunga, the Man Pack have cast
me out. I did them no harm, but they were
afraid of me. Why?

Wolf Pack, ye have cast me out too. The jungle is shut to me and the village gates are shut. Why?

As Mang flies between the beasts and the birds so fly I between the village and the jungle. Why?

I dance on the hide of Shere Khan, but my heart is very heavy. My mouth is cut and wounded with the stones from the village, but my heart is very light because I have come back to the jungle. Why?

These two things fight together in me as the snakes fight in the spring. The water comes out of my eyes; yet I laugh while it falls. Why?

I am two Mowglis, but the hide of Shere Khan is under my feet.

All the jungle knows that I have killed Shere Khan. Look—look well, O Wolves!

Ahae! My heart is heavy with the things that I do not understand.